*A SECOND CHANCE
ROMANCE NOVEL*

Compass

NEW YORK TIMES BESTSELLING AUTHOR
DEBORAH BLADON

Also by Deborah Bladon

Chapter 1

Kate

"I'm thinking a mermaid style gown. It has to be sleek and fitted. That's exactly what I want, Kate."

That's not what she wants. Corly Brunton has come to my bridal shop every week for the past month to try on dresses. Three weeks ago it was mermaid style and those were all thumbs down from the group of four bridesmaids she brought with her.

Two weeks ago she was convinced that she wanted a princess ball gown. Last week, she went through an off-white, off-the-shoulder phase.

"I think Natalie has the perfect dress in mind for you," I say, laughing inwardly because I know my assistant manager is going to be pissed that I'm dragging her into this.

"I love Natalie," Corly claps her hands together. "I'm ready whenever she is."

I slip out of the change room and set out to find Natalie Diehl.

Katie Rose Bridal is busier than usual today. I attribute that to the fact that a member of the royal family tied the knot just a few days ago.

Whenever a high profile wedding takes over the headlines, business picks up.

"Natalie," I call out to her when I see her red hair peek out from behind a rack of vintage dresses in the stock room.

"What do you need, Kate?" she asks, glancing over to where I'm standing.

"I need you to grab the A-line gown that came in yesterday that you thought would be perfect for Corly Brunton."

"The lace one with beading on the bodice?" Natalie rests her hand on her hip. "Is she back?"

"She's in change room four and you're about to sell her that gown." I skim my hand over the front of my red sheath dress. "I thought you'd appreciate the commission on the sale."

She narrows her eyes. "I see right through you, Kate Wesley. As much as I would love to help Corly not find the perfect dress again, I'm busy with a bride of my own."

"I can take over that."

She scratches her chin. "This bride's budget is more than Corly's. I'm talking way more, Kate."

"The commission on both is yours, even if I make the sale."

"I'm game." She starts walking across the room. "I'll grab the dress for Corly and you'll go help Annalise Brookings find her perfect gown."

"She's in the main showroom?"

Natalie nods. "With her entourage of seven. Her fiancé and his best man are on the way too."

When I first started working in bridal, I was surprised whenever a future groom showed up to witness his soon-to-be wife trying on dresses. It's not that uncommon. We have at least a few men in the showroom every week.

"What's Annalise looking for in a gown?"

"I don't have a clue." Natalie laughs as she zips open the garment bag on the A-line gown. "We haven't gotten that far yet. I came back here to get a new notepad and a pen so I could jot down what she likes."

"I'm about to find out." I smile as I turn toward the doorway. "Wish me luck."

I take quick steps down the carpeted corridor that leads to the main showroom of Katie Rose Bridal.

I had it redecorated two years ago in elegant and sophisticated tones. The benches are covered in cream-colored fabrics. The walls are painted pale gray. It's the perfect space to choose a dress to wear on the most important day of your life.

A client walking back toward the change rooms catches my eye. I glance at the gown she's trying on. It has a sweetheart neckline and a lace train. It's a beautiful dress that has brought a tear to her eye.

This is exactly why I bought this boutique.

"You look stunning," I whisper to her as we pass each other.

I round the corner to the showroom and spot a group of women huddled together.

One of the women is staring in a mirror while the others gather around her. The tiara on her head is a clear sign that she's the bride-to-be.

I smile as I near her. "You must be Annalise."

"That's me." She shakes with excitement. "I'm here to find my wedding dress."

"I'm Kate." I reach out to take her hand in mine. "I'm excited to help you do just that."

"You have perfect timing, Kate." Her hand flies in the air next to my shoulder. "My man is here with his best man."

I turn to face the double glass doors that open onto the sidewalk in front of the boutique.

Time stops.

My breath catches.

I stare at the two men in suits walking toward us.

One is blond with a beard and a blank look on his face as he takes in the dresses, veils, and vases of fresh flowers that decorate the boutique.

The other man is the one I can't take my eyes off of.

His hair is brown, his eyes a shade of green I'll never forget and the smile on his face could still light the night sky.

He slows as he nears me, his hand reaching up to touch his chest.

"Katie?" His voice rumbles through me as deeply as it did the first time I heard it.

I nod, my head moving as slow as time had when he left me days before our wedding with little explanation and a broken heart.

"Gage," I say his name softly. "Gage Burke."

Chapter 2

Kate

"*Time heals all wounds.*"

The words my mom said to me the day Gage left me echo through my mind.

That was five years ago.

I've held fast to the faith that those words are true, but if time heals all wounds, seeing an ex-fiancé rips them open until they're gaping and raw.

"You know Gage?" Annalise shakes my arm as if that's going to jerk me out of my daze.

It doesn't work.

I stand and stare at the man I thought I'd build a lifetime of memories with.

I loved him for more than two years and I never saw him dressed like this.

His suit is dark blue. The tie around his neck is as white as his dress shirt.

Dr. Gage Burke.

That was his dream. Maybe, just maybe his dreams came true.

"It was forever ago," I manage to say as I turn to look at her.

Is she his fiancée?

I drop my gaze to her left hand and the massive emerald cut diamond on her finger.

I rub the back of my ring finger with my thumb.

It's bare. I took the silver band with the blue topaz stone off of my finger the day Gage called off our engagement.

I handed it back to him. He insisted I keep it. I suggested he go to hell.

"Katie." His breath gusts over the back of my neck.

My hand moves to cover the skin that's exposed. I gathered my long blonde hair up into a ponytail this morning after I brushed my teeth.

I put on my makeup, got dressed and came to work as if this would be a day like every other.

I couldn't have known the earth would crack open and my past would come crawling out.

"You're in New York," Gage says from behind me.

I've thought about his voice endlessly. I replayed the last voicemail message he left me over and over until I deleted it before I stepped on the airplane the day I moved to Manhattan.

"Obviously." Annalise rolls her eyes. "Her name is on the front of the store. Can you two catch up later? I need to find a dress so I can marry Myles."

My traitorous heart leaps inside my chest.

Myles is her fiancé, not Gage.

"I'm Myles Sims." The blond-haired man shoves a hand at me. "It's good to meet you, Kate."

With a tentative hand, I reach for his.

He holds it for a moment too long as if he knows. I look up into his blue eyes. They're kind and understanding. Impatience doesn't live there.

"Are you sure you have time for us today?" He holds my hand in his. "I booked the appointment myself with a woman named Natalie."

He's giving me an out. I have no idea why, but I take it with a squeeze of his hand in appreciation. "Natalie will be right here."

"You're not helping me?" Annalise's bottom lip juts out in a pout.

"Kate must have a million things on her plate, darling." Myles drops my hand to run his finger over Annalise's lip. "Natalie will help us. Besides, I see your dream dress right over there."

"Where?" Annalise's head snaps to the left and then the right.

Myles guides her chin to the center of the boutique. "Over there. That's the dress from Kate's website."

Annalise takes off in the direction of the vintage Chanel gown that's been sitting in a glass showcase for more than a year. The price tag is too steep for most of Manhattan, but a picture of it on the front page of my website lures brides-to-be through the door.

"Let's go, Gage." Myles's voice resonates behind me.

I don't turn around.

There's no need for me to steal another glance at the man I once loved. I can draw from memory every inch of his handsome face. I can still smell the scent of his skin when I close my eyes, just as I can hear the ache in the growl he makes when he orgasms.

Gage Burke was once as much a part of me as my beating heart.

He's not anymore. He never will be again.

Chapter 3

Gage

Kate Wesley.
My Katie Wesley.
I stare at her back as she walks out of the showroom, disappearing down a long corridor.

I followed Myles to this bridal shop today out of a sense of duty.

He asked me to be his best man the day after he proposed to Annalise. That was two months after he sat down on a barstool and poured his heart out to me.

I returned the favor by telling him about Katie.

When drowning his sorrow in beer stopped working, he looked to Annalise to help him forget the woman who had loved and left him.

It's worked out well for him.

I yank on the tie around my neck.

I can't remember the last time I wore a tie or a suit, for that matter.

The one on my back is courtesy of Myles. He took me to his tailor three weeks ago to get fitted for this.

I pulled out my credit card, but Myles insisted that it was on his dime. I scoffed, but he's sparing no expense on this wedding so I'll arrange a bachelor party he won't soon forget.

The knot loosens and I breathe a sigh of relief.

I have no idea if the tie is what's suffocating me or if seeing Katie is forcing all the air out of my lungs.

I finally break the tie's grip on my neck enough that I can undo the top button of my shirt.

I'm a walking mannequin at the moment since Annalise has to sign off on what I'm wearing.

I'll put on the suit one more time on the day of their wedding. After that, I'll hand it off to someone who needs it more than I do.

"I'm liking the look, Gage." Annalise points at me. "Don't mess up that tie. The silk is imported from Italy."

Priorities in Annalise's world don't mirror my own.

She's a beauty by most men's measure. Her brunette hair falls to the middle of her back. Her blue eyes are bold. Her face has landed on more than one fashion magazine.

She's the dream that Myles needs to settle his past once and for all.

My past just walked out of this showroom in the form of a blonde-haired, hazel-eyed, spitfire of a woman.

"Everyone sit down," Annalise demands with a sweep of her hand in the air toward a large curved bench. "I'm about to wow you with this gown."

I had my wow moment.

Katie Wesley is hiding somewhere in this boutique and now that I know she's here, nothing is going to stop me from righting the wrongs of my past.

***

"Are you running for mayor?" Zeke Morrow gives me the once-over. "If you are, don't count on my vote."

"What the fuck?" I toss my hands in the air in mock shock. "If I can't count on one of my closest friends, who the hell can I count on?"

"There's a cute brunette at table seven eyeing you up." He gestures past my shoulder. "I bet you can count on her vote and an invitation to her place."

I don't bother stealing a glance at the woman he's talking about.

Since I bought this bar, there hasn't been a shortage of women wanting to take me home.

I don't fuck customers. I leave that to Zeke.

He tends bar, does the books and when the urge strikes him, he'll spend the night with a woman who wanders into Tin Anchor looking for more than a drink.

"What's with the suit?" He pushes his eyeglasses up the bridge of his nose. "That's expensive, no?"

"Very." I nod as I finally pocket the tie.

After wedding dress shopping, I was invited to Nova, Annalise's favorite restaurant.

I tried to bow out with an excuse about needing to relieve Zeke behind the bar, but Myles convinced me to sit through the celebratory champagne toast.

I took off before the appetizer round left the kitchen.

"Myles picked it out," I go on, tapping my hand on the top of the wooden bar. "It's what the best man wears in his world."

Zeke fingers the collar of the jacket. "This is premium. Myles spared no expense for his favorite guy."

I swat his hand away with a laugh. "Your brother is building his Wall Street wardrobe, right? We're about the same size. It's his after the wedding if he wants it."

"You're fucking joking."

"Dead serious," I shoot back. "Myles knows I'm paying it forward after they tie the knot. If Grady wants it, it's his."

"He wants it." He rakes a hand through his dark hair. "He'll buy you a bottle of scotch to thank you."

I point at the array of bottles on one of the shelves behind the bar. "I've got the scotch covered. He can let me beat him in pool the next time we play."

"Deal." Zeke looks over at a group of guys who just walked in. "I'm back at it. You hanging out here for the night?"

I look around. We're busy, but Zeke has it covered. "I just stopped in to see if you needed me, but looks like I'm taking the night off."

"Enjoy," Zeke says as he walks away.

I'll enjoy it more if I can track Katie down. I haven't stopped thinking about her since I saw her this afternoon. Hell, I haven't been able to get her off of my mind for more than two minutes in the past five years.

She's a woman no man in his right mind could ever forget.

Chapter 4

Kate

I walk into Premier Pet Care and stare across the reception desk at my best friend, Tilly Wolf.

Her blue eyes skim my face. "What's going on?"

I bring my hand to my lips and shake my head.

Tilly's gaze darts to the waiting room. "I have to help Dr. Hunt. He's going to clip that poodle's nails. After that, I'm off the clock. Are we talking cheeseburger or martini?"

It's our sliding scale when something is wrong in my world.

Tilly's life has settled since she found her prince charming in the form of a black-haired police sergeant named Sebastian Wolf.

If Tilly isn't with her husband, she's working here as a vet assistant or hanging out with me.

"Both," I spit out as I look down at the silver watch on my wrist. "Should I sit in the waiting room until you're done?"

"No." A man's voice from the left startles me. "You should drag Matilda out of here now. I owe her a few minutes since she stayed late last night."

Dr. Donovan Hunt tosses me a mega-watt smile.

He's Tilly's boss and clearly the type of all the women who flock here to have him check out their cats, dogs, and whatever other creatures he can cure with his magic touch.

Tilly wanted to set me up with him once until I pointed out the obvious to her.

I don't want her working with a potential ex of mine.

I like my friendship with Tilly just as it is and that's drama free.

"I can leave?" Tilly asks as she rounds the reception desk with her bag slung over her shoulder. "You'll handle Finn on your own?"

The poodle barks at the mention of his name.

"Kate looks like she needs a friend to lean on." Donovan nods at me. "I have a sister, so I know how it works."

I ignore what I think might have been a subtle insult about the way I look.

I glanced in the mirror in my office before I walked the two blocks over here. I know all the color has drained from my face.

That happens when the man you once loved strolls back into your life five years after he trampled all over your heart.

"I'll see you tomorrow, Dr. Hunt." Tilly tosses him a wave over her shoulder.

"Take good care of Kate," he offers with a friendly grin.

I manage a small smile back as Tilly grabs my hand and steers me out of the clinic.

***

An hour later, we're on the sofa in my apartment. Tilly traded her blue scrubs for a pair of my sweatpants and a red T-shirt. I'm dressed in black yoga shorts and a yellow tank top.

We're both looking down at our plates on the coffee table and the scraps of what used to be two cheeseburgers and a shared order of fries.

We splurged on delivery because we saved money by not going to a bar to order martinis.

Tilly sips on the glass of water in her hand as she glances at me. "Sebastian is having dinner with his brothers, so I can hang out all night. You don't have to tell me what's going on, Kate, but I'm here for you."

Since Tilly and I met, she's been one of the most supportive friends I have.

I include my friend, Olivia Donato, in that category too. Her time right now is spent doting on her four-month-old daughter, Arleth.

"Someone came into the boutique today." I tread lightly to give my heart time to ready for the words I have to say aloud.

"More than one someone I hope." Tilly smiles, twirling a strand of her long brown hair around her finger. "You can't keep the doors open with one customer a day."

I know she's trying to lighten the mood because my sullen silence through dinner wasn't normal. Usually, I can't shut up about what's going on at work.

"Who was it?" Her hand reaches for mine.

I glance down at the simple silver band on her ring finger. Tilly and Sebastian eloped in Mexico. When they first told me, I had to hide the disappointment on my face. I wanted to help Tilly choose a perfect gown and plan the wedding of her dreams.

Once she described their intimate beach wedding to me, I understood everything.

They followed their hearts and it took them to that spot as the ocean water kissed their bare feet and they exchanged vows.

Maybe if Gage and I hadn't planned a celebration to please three hundred other people things would have been different. Maybe they would have turned out exactly as they did.

Questioning the past is a fool's pursuit.

That's another gem courtesy of my mom.

"Tell me who was at the boutique, Kate." Tilly leans closer to me, a soft smile on her lips.

I say his name, trying to keep my voice from trembling. "Gage."

Her brow furrows as she processes what I just said. "Gage? Your Gage?"

He hasn't been my Gage in forever and after he left, I questioned if he ever was.

My silence spurs Tilly on. "Are you saying you saw Gage Burke today? He was at Katie Rose? He was at your boutique?"

I nod slowly. "He was there. In the flesh."

"Fuck." The word leaves her lips slowly. "This is huge. I want every detail."

Chapter 5

Kate

"You sold the Chanel?" Tilly's eyebrows jump up. "Why are we not drinking champagne tonight and feasting on escargot?"

"Ew." I scrunch my nose at the mention of snails.

I probably shouldn't have opened my story with the sale of the Chanel gown, but I was trying to ease myself into talking about Gage.

"None of that matters," Tilly goes on with a shake of her head. "Where does Gage fit into this?"

"He's the best man in that wedding." I almost laugh at the irony of my words.

Gage would always tell me he was the best man; for me, for the job of pediatrician, for the task of cooking me his infamous baked shrimp scampi every Sunday night.

"Is this wedding taking place in Manhattan?" Tilly asks with a tilt of her head.

I didn't bother asking the question.

After Myles gave me a way out of the appointment, I found Natalie on her way into Corly's change room with the A-line dress in hand. I grabbed it from her, giving her a weak explanation about needing her to take over with Annalise. She told me she'd do it.

I know she could see the emotion swimming in my eyes. The brief hug she gave me said more than any words she could have offered.

She went to the showroom, secured the sale of the Chanel gown and left the boutique at the end of the day with a huge smile and a big paycheck coming her way.

"Is he living in New York?" Tilly's eyes widen. "Is that possible?"

After seeing Gage's face today, I'd say anything is possible. "I don't know."

She reaches for her phone. She dropped it on the coffee table after calling her husband to tell him she'd be late getting home tonight. "When's the last time you searched for Gage online?"

I shrug my shoulders. "It's been years."

She tosses me a skeptical glance. "Years, Kate?"

"Years, Tilly," I answer honestly.

Gage may have owned every one of my thoughts after he left, but when I deleted his voicemail, I swore to myself I'd leave my pain back in Los Angeles.

It's been hard, but I've resisted the urge to seek out any information about him since that day. It's not because my curiosity has taken a hike. It's because I'm fearful that I'll stumble on a social media profile belonging to him that features a picture of him with another woman.

My heart is strong, but there's a limit to what it can bear.

"He's a doctor, I think." I hold up a hand to ward off the question I know is about to leave Tilly's lips. "I didn't find that online. He was dressed in an expensive suit today. Gage never wore suits and his dream was to be a pediatrician, so I'm connecting the dots."

She glances up from her phone. "Those dots don't connect, Kate."

I scratch the back of my hand, anxiety nipping at me. "What do you mean?"

"Gage Burke owns a bar in Greenwich Village." There's a pause before she continues, "The Tin Anchor. That's the name of his bar."

I stare at her, replaying every word she just said in my mind.

Gage owns a bar in New York City?

This was supposed to be my safe place.

I came here after my mom's best friend offered me a job working in her bridal salon. It didn't fit with my business degree, but I didn't care. I craved a fresh start and a job clear across the country was just what I needed.

My family thought I was torturing myself. They couldn't understand why I chose to sell bridal gowns to pay my bills since I never had a chance to wear the one I picked out for myself.

Watching the dreams of other women come true was exactly what I needed at the time. I was forced to push my sorrow aside since all of my focus had to be on helping someone else find the perfect dress for the day they would say their forever vows.

"We should take a trip to Greenwich Village." Tilly raises a fist in the air. "We'll give him a piece of our minds."

"No." I drag myself to my feet, picking up the empty plates as I do. "I'm not going anywhere near Tin Anchor."

"Can I?" She wiggles her brows. "I have a few choice words for that man."

Everything Tilly knows about Gage came straight out of my mouth in a moment of despair. I've only ever talked about him when I've felt the weight of my broken heart was too much for me to carry.

It's been months since I've mentioned him to her or Olivia and just as long since I deleted the last picture I had of him on my phone. It was our engagement photo and when I showed it to Tilly soon after we met, I could see pity in her eyes.

"Don't waste your time." I start toward my kitchen. "The past has no place in the present."

"Let me guess." Tilly jumps to her feet to follow me. "Your mom said that to you."

"I came up with that jewel myself."

"Here's a jewel of my own." Tilly steps in place next to me at my sink. "Your past is part of your present and he knows where you work."

I turn to look at her. "You think Gage is going to come back to the boutique?"

"I guarantee it." She rinses her plate under the tap water. "Tomorrow."

"Tomorrow?" I take the plate from her and put it in the dishwasher.

"Mark my words." She leans her hip against the counter. "Today he realized what he lost. He'll do everything he can to find your heart again."

I look down at my chest. "My heart is smarter than that."

"Your head is." She taps my forehead with her finger. "Hearts are another matter and from what you've told me, Gage Burke still owns a piece of yours."

"He doesn't." I laugh off her words.

"You can lie to me if you want, Kate." She smiles. "You can't lie to your heart."

She's right.

Gage still owns a piece of my heart, but the time has come for me to take it back, once and for all.

Chapter 6

Gage

I rest one foot on the bench and stare out over the East River.

This is the reward for my daily pre-dawn pilgrimage since I moved to Manhattan.

The sunrise from this spot is fucking amazing even when low fog blankets the city as it is now.

Some days, I make the trek on foot, like I did today. Other mornings, I bike here to enjoy the peace that this spot offers before the city wakes and grinds up to full speed.

New York City is as far from the serenity of open water as a man can get, but I'm learning its charm is unique.

"It's beautiful, isn't it?"

I turn at the sound of a familiar voice behind me.

"Gus," I flash him a smile. "You made it today."

Gray-haired Gus was sitting on this bench the first day I wandered down here. He didn't offer a last name. I didn't ask.

All I know about him is that he's a native New Yorker with a tarnished band on his ring finger and a thousand stories about the woman he loved.

"Lois favored days like this." He waves his wooden cane in the air. "Fog is for the fearless she'd tell me."

Lois, his late wife, was fearless, just as Katie is.

I tossed and turned the night away thinking about her.

I checked out the website for her boutique, Katie Rose Bridal, as soon as I got home last night.

It opens at ten a.m., and I plan to be at the door at nine fifty-five.

"Where's your mind today, Gage?" Gus lowers himself to the bench.

I shift my stance, dropping my hands to my hips. "On a shower."

He laughs, taking in the running shorts I'm wearing and the sweat pouring down my forehead.

"Lois ran a half marathon once. Did I ever tell you that?"

Twice, but I'll listen again if he's in the mood.

"She placed second." He waves two fingers in the air; both are curled from the wear of arthritis on his joints. "I was waiting at the finish line with a dozen red roses."

Then he dropped to one knee and slid a diamond on her finger.

He doesn't finish the story. A helicopter overhead catches his attention.

"I'm taking off." I reach forward to pat his shoulder. "I'll see you tomorrow?"

"God willing you will." He laughs. "Make today count, Gage."

I plan on it.

***

Sticking to the plan will only take you so far. For me, that's the showroom floor at Katie Rose Bridal.

"Is she here?" I ask the question for a second time. "Has Katie come to work yet?"

"As I told you already, Kate is unavailable at the moment," Natalie says to me.

I thought she'd grant me some insight into when I can talk to Katie since we spent a large part of our afternoon together yesterday.

She helped Annalise into a gown and for the next hour I sat on a bench listening to the maid-of-honor and the bridesmaids tell her that the dress was made for her.

Natalie tossed me a sympathetic look after the first thirty minutes. Today, I'm getting nothing from her but a brick wall being thrown in my way.

"I'm an old friend of Katie's." I shove a hand into the pocket of my jeans to slide out my phone. "I've got a great photo of her when she was in college."

Her eyes drop to my phone as I scroll through the album that holds more pictures of Katie than I can count.

Natalie's hand lands on mine to stop me. "She called this morning and said she'd be late. I have no idea if or when she'll show up, Gage."

I exhale. "I'll drop back in this afternoon."

"Good idea." She looks past me when the door to the boutique opens. "That's my first appointment of the day."

I glance over my shoulder at a petite blonde woman holding a bridal magazine.

If owning a store like this was Katie's dream, she kept it hidden from me.

The woman I fell in love with aspired to take over her dad's company. She wanted to see her name on the door of the CEO's office at Wesley Pharmaceuticals in Los Angeles.

I look back at Natalie. "How long has Katie owned this place?"

"I'm not sure." She shrugs a shoulder. "She hired me a little over a year ago. If you'll excuse me, I really do need to get to my bride-to-be."

"Don't let me keep you." I glance down at my watch. "When you see Katie, tell her I'll be back."

"I'll do that," she says cheerfully.

I take my leave and step out onto the sidewalk outside the boutique. I have no idea if Katie is avoiding me, but sooner or later I'm going to come face-to-face with her. If I have my way it will be this afternoon.

Chapter 7

Kate

"One down and thousands left to go, Kate or should I say Katie?" Natalie asks as she walks into my office.

"Kate." I sigh. "One down and thousands of what left to go?"

"Days." She taps her watch. "You successfully avoided your old flame for today. What's the approach we're taking tomorrow? Are you going to be busy washing your hair? Or did your dog eat all the invoices?"

"I don't own a dog," I point out with a smile. "I thought dogs were partial to homework. That's what I remember from middle school."

"They'll eat anything as long as it keeps their owners occupied." She narrows her eyes. "You can borrow my dog."

"I'm good." I close the appointment calendar on my computer. "I don't think he'll be back tomorrow."

"He'll be back."

I rub a hand over my forehead. "Did he tell you that?"

"He didn't have to." She shakes her head. "He's anxious to talk to you. I have no idea what went down between you two, but I know from experience sometimes it's best to put the past to rest by having one last conversation with an ex."

I've never talked to Natalie about Gage. Our relationship borders on friendship, but we're not close.

"Sometimes, it's best to avoid the ex," I counter. "He'll give up eventually."

Just like he did five years ago.

I don't say those words even though they're playing on the tip of my tongue.

"You can't hide back here forever, Kate." She's right.

When I finally came in at noon, I ducked into my office to take care of a few calls. Natalie followed on my heel to tell me that Gage was waiting at the door when the boutique opened. He promised her he'd be back after lunch.

By the time he arrived just before two o'clock, I was knee deep in a delivery problem and told Natalie to show him the door.

He left forty-five minutes later.

I pulled up the security camera on my computer and watched him stroll out of the boutique.

The video was grainy, but I could tell that he showed up here in a pair of jeans and a white V-neck sweater. He was dressed the same way on the day we met eight years ago.

I was only nineteen-years-old.

He was twenty-one.

Time has been kind to his body. The cut of his expensive suit showcased that.

The last time I saw him he wasn't as muscular as he is now. His hips and waist weren't as trim.

"I'm going to go home and make my husband dinner." Natalie studies me for a minute. "I know Gage hurt you, Kate. I can see it. I want you to know that I'll run interference for as long as it takes but facing pain can be cathartic."

Or it can be debilitating.

I won't let Gage's sudden appearance in my life undo all the strides I've made.

"I'll see you tomorrow, Nat."

"You bet, Katie." She winks. "I'll be here bright and early."

I can't promise the same.

***

Mom: *What's the what?*

I laugh as I read my mom's text message.

Kate: *I'm making dinner.*

Her reply is instant, which is surprising since my mom is always telling me texting is her least favorite way to communicate with me. She prefers phone calls or very long emails.

I like text messages because we can get to the point in no time flat.

Mom: *Making dinner or putting take-out on a plate?*

I look down at the sushi I picked up on my way home.

Kate: *Busted.*

As she types back a reply, I pop a spicy salmon roll in my mouth. I tap the chopstick on the side of the take-out container as I chew.

Mom: *Invite me to NYC and I'll cook all your favorites. You must miss my meatloaf.*

I miss sitting on the wooden stool in her kitchen watching her make it. It was our regular Wednesday afternoon routine when I was in grade school. I'd do my homework by the table and she'd gather together all the ingredients for the best meatloaf I've ever had.

Kate: *I miss the meatloaf and you.*

I know my mom. Her eyes are misting with tears as she reads the text message I just sent.

Both of her kids have set out to live their own lives. My older brother, Eldred, and his wife settled in California. They're a two-hour drive from my folks' house. I'm a five-hour plane ride away.

Mom: *Say the word and I'll buy a ticket for the meatloaf and me.*

My mom would know exactly what I should do about Gage. She'd coach me through all of it, but I'm not the same twenty-two-year-old woman who was left by her fiancé just days before their wedding.

I can do this. I need to do this on my own.

Taking a sip of lemon water, my gaze drops when another text message pops up on the screen of my phone.

Mom: *I'm there if you need me.*

I smile at the offer.

Kate: *I always need you, but let's save the trip for your birthday.*

It's months away and by then, I'll have put my past with Gage to rest and my mom will never have to know that he stumbled back into my life.

Our break-up was hard on me, but I saw the impact it had on my parents.

They gave Gage their blessing when he asked for my hand in marriage. My dad tried to hide the tears in his eyes when I told him that there would be no walk down the aisle. My mom wept when we donated my wedding dress.

Mom: *This year I'll turn 40 for the 15th time, so a trip to New York is the perfect way to celebrate. Eat all your take-out and brush your teeth. Love you.*

Laughing, I shake my head.

Kate: *Love you too.*

Chapter 8

Gage

My fingers roll over the black stone beads on the bracelet that's been on my left wrist for almost seven years.

I glance down at it.

It's a part of me now. I can't picture my arm without it.

A tap on my shoulder draws my gaze back to a guy in a black T-shirt, dark jeans and a shaved head. "You're loitering. You need to get lost."

"You don't own the sidewalk," I point out. "I'm waiting for someone."

"Your bride?" he questions as he lights a cigarette he pulled out of his back pocket. "You haven't taken your eyes off the wedding dress shop since you parked your ass here."

Technically, it's my feet that are parked in this spot.

I'm leaning against a lamppost outside of a record store.

Who the fuck knew that records were still so popular? He's had a steady stream of customers since he unlocked the door thirty minutes ago.

"Are your feet cold?" The guy asks with a laugh.

I look down at my shoes. They're black leather oxfords that paired well with the dark jeans and white dress shirt I'm wearing.

I rolled the sleeves of the shirt up to my elbows because it's hot as hell out.

I'm trying to make a good impression, although Katie never gave a shit about what was on my back.

Your heart is the most beautiful in the world, Gage.

Her words, not mine.

She said them for the last time five years ago. I doubt they'll ever leave her lips again.

"You're not the first guy to hang out here because of a case of cold feet." He taps the cigarette sending the ash to the sidewalk. "I always tell guys like you the same thing."

He has no idea what kind of man I am, but I listen because his voice is better than silence right now.

I spent all night in the darkness of my apartment replaying the day I broke Katie's heart.

His hand brushes my shoulder as he points across the street at Katie's boutique. "If you need to take a breather here, you don't belong over there."

"I'm not getting married," I say with a quick glance in his direction.

"Wise man." He drops the cigarette, smashing the toe of his black boot into it.

I'm a wiser man now than I was five years ago.

My gaze wanders to a beautiful blonde in a light blue dress headed toward the boutique. Her hair is loose. The gentle waves are bouncing around her shoulders.

She's as breathtaking this morning as she was the first time I saw her on the campus at UCLA.

"Katie," I say her name under my breath as my fingers play over my bracelet.

"My break is over." The guy from the record store pats my back. "Good luck, man."

I don't need luck. I need forgiveness.

***

By the time I'm at the door of the boutique, Katie's inside.

I peer through the glass and watch her talking to a woman wearing a wedding dress.

From my view of Katie's profile, I can see the smile on her face. I've never forgotten that smile.

The left side of her mouth inches up slightly higher than the right when she's grinning ear-to-ear.

I used to do everything in my power to earn a smile like that from her.

"Excuse me." A woman brushes past me on her way into the store.

I follow on her heel, hoping to hell that Katie won't glance over, spot me, and take off in a sprint to a place I can't reach her.

"You're beaming," Katie reaches for the hand of the woman in the wedding gown. "Your grandmother's veil is going to look perfect with this gown."

Her voice is just as I remember it. It's soft and soothing. She used to read aloud in bed before we'd fall asleep. It was mostly poetry, words written by others that captured what was in her heart.

The last gift I ever gave her was a book inscribed to her by her favorite poet.

She was at a loss for words when she ripped the gift open. The only thing I had to wrap the book in was newspaper I found in the hallway outside our apartment and a pink ribbon tucked in one of her dresser drawers.

"*This is beautiful,*" she said at the time.

It was the effort I put in that was beautiful to her, not the day old newspaper or the fraying ribbon.

"What do you think?" The bride-to-be's gaze shifts from Katie to me. "I'd love a man's honest opinion on this gown."

She spins in a circle as Katie turns to face me.

The smile on her face flees as quickly as the pain in her eyes appears.

"Katie," I say her name not thinking about what comes next.

"What do you think?" The woman in the dress repeats. "Will my fiancé think I'm the most beautiful woman in the world when he sees me walk down the aisle in this?"

I ignore her as I stare into the face of the woman who promised her heart to me on her twenty-first birthday when I dropped to one knee and asked her to spend her life with me.

"I'm sorry, Katie," I say what I've held inside since I told her that I couldn't marry her.

Her gaze falls to my mouth before she locks eyes with me. Her voice comes out in a whisper. "You should go."

I should. I'm a fucking asshole for waltzing in here and blurting out the words that should have left my mouth years ago. I could have kept them inside until we weren't next to a stranger and surrounded by hundreds of wedding gowns.

I nod. "I'll go."

She turns on her heel and I leave her store knowing that a weak apology can never make up for the devastation I've caused.

I hope to hell I can find a way to explain what tore me away from the life we had planned together.

Chapter 9

Kate

I walk into my bedroom and pick up a soft white blanket. I hold it close to my face and inhale the sweet fragrance.

"Arleth smells like heaven, doesn't she?" Olivia asks from behind me. "Sometimes I catch Alexander with his nose in her little neck just inhaling that perfect baby scent."

I laugh as I turn to face her. "Your husband is a smart man. Arleth is a little peach."

Olivia reaches for the blanket. She tossed it on my bed along with her purse and Arleth's diaper bag when she got here an hour ago.

Since then, we've been waiting for Tilly to get off of work.

Olivia fed Arleth while I took a quick shower and changed into ripped jeans and a white tank top.

I pulled Tilly and Olivia into a group text message after Gage left the boutique this morning.

It was their joint idea to spend the evening together. Olivia brought sparkling water for herself and a big salad with roasted chicken to share. Tilly is picking up a bottle of white wine for her and me.

"I put Arleth down in that little travel bed you had tucked in your front closet." She smiles. "I think she's beginning to like it more than her crib at home."

I picked up the travel bed soon after Arleth was born. I thought Olivia could use it when she goes to visit her husband at the music school he runs. It turns out, Alexander bought a crib for his office there, so the travel bed is in my apartment ready to be put to use whenever Olivia brings her daughter over.

"I set up the bed close to the window." Olivia sighs. "I swear that little angel loves sunshine more than she loves me."

I smile. "I love how happy you are."

Her blue eyes brighten. "Life is good. I'm a very lucky woman."

She deserves everything life has gifted her with including her wonderful husband, baby daughter and the job she loves. She's on maternity leave now, but in a few weeks she'll go back to her executive position at Liore Lingerie, and Alexander will take Arleth to the music school with him.

"I want you to be happy too, Kate." She brushes a strand of her brown hair behind her shoulder. "I know how much it upset you seeing Gage this morning."

It was jarring. I didn't know he was in the boutique until I turned around and saw his face.

A thousand different emotions collided inside of me all at once. I wanted to scream at him, drop to my knees in sorrow and run out the door. I didn't do any of those things.

I told him to go. I've waited five years to hear him say he was sorry, and yet when the words left his lips, the pain inside of me didn't dissipate at all.

"I still can't believe he's in New York." I pinch my eyes shut. "I thought I'd never see him again and now we're living in the same city."

A chime from my cell pulls my gaze over my shoulder to my nightstand. I dropped my phone there when I took off the dress I was wearing before my shower. "That's probably Tilly. I'll buzz her up."

"We'll get you through this." Olivia hugs her baby's blanket to her chest. "Tilly, Arleth, and I are your crew. We have food and wine. What more do you need?"

Peace.

I had it before Gage showed up and now that I know he's in New York, the confusion that enveloped me after he walked out of my life five years ago has wrapped itself back around me.

***

"If I were you, I'd call Preston and fuck his brains out."

Tilly and I both look over at Olivia. It's not that she doesn't curse, but a statement that bold hasn't left her mouth since she gave birth to Arleth.

Dinner was delicious. The conversation focused on Tilly's day at the vet clinic. After Olivia fed Arleth again, she put her down to sleep, and the discussion took a sharp turn in the direction of Gage Burke.

Tilly weighed in first. Her advice was typical Tilly. She told me to set up a meeting with him, talk through what took him away from me five years ago, and see if the spark is still there.

I brushed that idea off with a swallow of wine and a roll of my eyes.

Olivia's advice is obviously not what I expected.

"You want me to what with Preston?"

Olivia dips her index finger into the balled fist of her left hand. She slides it in and out slowly.

I almost choke on my wine. "What the hell are you doing?"

"What do you think I'm doing?" She laughs. "I think you should finally have sex with Preston."

"Finally?" Tilly grabs my forearm in a death grip. "You've been on three dates with him, Kate. Are you telling me that you haven't slept with him yet?"

"We kissed," I say flatly.

Tilly, Olivia, and I were at a café on Broadway and Seventy-Fourth a month ago. Preston Metcalfe was standing in line behind me. He flirted with me. I responded in kind.

He's good-looking with a strong, tall build, and a job in finance.

More importantly, he's single and interested in me.

We've had lunch once since then and dinner twice.

We agreed at the café before he took my number, that we would take things slow.

So far, we've both stuck to that promise. Things are moving at a snail's pace since we've only kissed a few times.

He hinted that he wanted to go down on me after our last dinner when he said I looked like the most delicious dessert he's ever seen, but then his phone rang. Someone's financial emergency stole him away before he could get a first taste.

"You kissed his cock?" Tilly says with a half-grin. "That's what you're saying, right?"

"You knew Sebastian for weeks before you jumped into bed with him," I point out with a lift of my empty wine glass in the air. "This is a no judgment zone, Tilly."

"He was my roommate," she says in a rush. "It's completely different."

"You and the sergeant are yesterday's news." Olivia pats Tilly's shoulder. "We're here to help Kate stay strong so Gage doesn't drive a bulldozer over her heart again."

"She needs to talk to him," Tilly insists. "They left things unsaid years ago. Until they clear the air, what they had will never be truly over."

"It was over when he took his parents' sailboat out on the Pacific." Olivia takes a deep breath. "He hasn't spent the past five years looking for her. A coincidence dropped him back into Kate's orbit. She doesn't owe him a thing, especially not another minute of her life."

Clearing my throat, I lean forward to tap my fingers on my small dining table. "I'm sitting right here. I get a say in what my next step should be, don't I?"

"Talk to him," Tilly reiterates.

"Call Preston and take it past first base." Olivia mimes swinging a baseball bat.

As if on cue, my phone starts ringing. Olivia jumps to her feet and runs toward my coffee table to scoop it up in her palm. Her gaze drops to the screen, a wide smile spreading across her face. "Speak of the handsome devil. Preston's ears must have been burning. He's calling and whatever he wants, say *yes*."

Chapter 10

Kate

I said yes.

Six years ago to Gage when he asked me to marry him and last night, I said it again on the phone to Preston when he suggested we meet for a drink after work today.

The pout on Tilly's face said it all.

She was not impressed with my decision to forgo her advice in favor of Olivia's.

I don't know if there's a future for Preston and me. I do know that Gage is part of my past and right now, I need to keep him there.

A knock at my office door draws my gaze up.

"Come in," I call out softly.

I know Natalie is on the other side. She locked up just now as I was changing into a black, sleeveless dress and matching heels.

I piled my hair on top of my head in a messy bun and fixed my make up, finishing up with a ruby red lip.

"Holy hell," Natalie says as she opens the door. "You look incredible, Kate."

I do a quick spin on my heel to give her the full view of my dress. "You like?"

"I love." She laughs. "I take it you have a hot date?"

"It's just a drink." I drop my lipstick in the black clutch purse on my desk. "I'm meeting him in twenty minutes."

"Gage?" she asks tentatively. "I'm all for showing an ex what he's missing, but this takes it to an entirely new level."

I take the compliment with a smile. "No, not him. It's someone else."

She scratches the back of her neck. "He's a lucky man."

Preston called himself the same when I agreed to meet him tonight. He's uncomplicated and our time together has been drama free. He's just what I need right now as I sort through whether or not I should drag myself through the muddy past I share with Gage.

You'll stumble if you keep looking at what's behind you.

The words my mom said to me before I left California to move to New York echo through me.

Preston is right in front of me, and he deserves my full attention tonight.

"Will I see you in the morning?" Natalie asks with a wink. "I have it covered if your date turns into a sleepover."

I point at the watch on my wrist. "I'll be here before ten."

"Don't rush on my account." She laughs. "I'm heading home to see the hubs. I hope you have as much fun tonight as I plan on having."

Holding in a giggle, I shake my head. "It's just a drink, Nat."

"Famous last words," she quips. "You never know what awaits outside this boutique."

***

Twenty minutes later, I'm locking the boutique's door when someone grabs my shoulder. The self-defense training my dad gave me before I left California kicks into high gear.

I turn quickly and jab my thumb into the eye socket of the person holding onto me.

"Christ, Katie." Gage's hand darts to his eye. "What the hell was that for?"

I bite back a giggle as I take in the sight of my ex-fiancé flinching in pain. "I thought you were trying to mug me."

"Seriously?" He shakes his head, his open eye raking me from head-to-toe.

I take some twisted pleasure in the fact that I look hot tonight even though he looks just as good.

He's wearing a lightweight, long-sleeved blue sweater and faded jeans.

"I was hoping we could talk." He gestures to the area behind him with his elbow. "I was at the record store and saw you leaving so I sprinted across the street."

I glance at the street and the four lanes of traffic whizzing past us. If he wants me to be impressed that he risked life and limb to get to me, he's going to be disappointed.

"I don't have time, Gage." My eyes drop to the watch on my wrist.

I'm supposed to meet Preston at a bar two blocks from here in five minutes. The need to get to him isn't as strong as my desire to get away from Gage.

He smells exactly as he did the last time I saw him in California. It's the scent of his favorite body wash. I'm hit with a sudden rush of memories of all the early mornings and late night showers we took together. Showers that were less about cleaning our bodies and more about pleasuring each other.

"You have a date," he states matter-of-factly. "With who?"

I cross my arms over my chest. "That's none of your business."

"Is it serious?"

Stubborn pride takes root deep inside of me. I'm not giving this man an inch or a crumb of information about my life. He lost that privilege when he ended our relationship with a weak explanation about why he couldn't marry me.

"*I can't do it, Katie.*"

It was as simple as that.

I replayed those words over and over again in my mind. They held no clues about what took him away from me. They were as empty as the silence between us after he said them.

I gave him back the ring and walked out of our apartment. By the time I returned two hours later, he was gone.

"Is he your boyfriend?" He pushes for more. "Or is it more serious than that?"

I watch as he lowers his hand, revealing the bloodshot eye beneath. I'm not a violent person, but I won't apologize for the poke in his eye. If it caused even a fraction of the pain that he caused me, it was warranted.

"We're not having this discussion." I tuck a strand of hair behind my ear. "I need to go."

"To him?" he asks, his voice thick with emotion.

I nod. "Yes, to him."

He steps aside, granting me a path to the sidewalk. "He's a lucky bastard."

You were the lucky bastard once. Now you're just a bastard.

I bite back the words, not wanting to lose control. "Goodbye, Gage."

He swallows hard. "Goodnight, Katie."

I walk as quickly as my feet will take me until I round the corner and once I do, I lean against the side of a brick building. Taking a deep breath, I rub my shaking hand over my forehead.

Chapter 11

Gage

I had no right to follow Katie, but that's what I do.

As soon as she disappears from my sight I set out after her. I have no intention of interfering in her plans, but the burning need inside of me to know what he looks like is driving my feet forward.

I stop dead in my tracks when I turn the corner. I expected her to be sprinting down the sidewalk, not leaning against the exterior wall of a theatre.

Her hand is on her forehead; her breaths are labored and rushed.

I inch back so she doesn't spot me.

The urge to go to her and take her in my arms is strong. That's never diminished. It wouldn't matter if five years or fifty years passed. This woman lives within me. She owns my heart to this day.

That won't change, whether an ocean or my foolish stupidity separates us.

I watch as she slides her phone from her purse, her gaze dropping to the screen.

It's next to her ear in an instant, her lips mouthing words that are rushed.

She looks around but doesn't spot me standing next to a group of women who are debating which romantic comedy they want to see.

Katie's eyes are focused on something closer; someone closer to her.

It's a man.

It's him.

His back is to me but his phone is against his ear too, and he's headed right to Katie.

She smiles at him.

It's not the same bright smile she used to give me, but it's enough of a grin that I can tell that this guy is something special under his expensive black suit.

She drops her phone back in her purse. His is in his jacket pocket before he's on her, and then his arms are around her, his lips pressing against her cheek.

I stand frozen in place watching a scene I never wanted to witness.

Rage consumes me.

I'm not pissed at the guy in the suit who is touching Katie. My anger is directed at myself. I'm the asshole who walked away from the beautiful blonde he can't take his eyes off. I'm the jerk who didn't tell her my truth back then.

I let her believe I didn't want her, even though she's the *only* woman on this earth that I've ever wanted.

His fingers slide down her bare arm until her hand is in his.

They set off down the sidewalk with him gazing down at her. His profile a reminder to me of what a smart man looks like.

If he hasn't fallen in love with Katie yet, he's on the edge.

It's impossible not to fall in love with the woman, and once a man does, he's lost to her for the rest of his life.

I should know.

***

"The rain doesn't slow you down, Gage."

I look over at Gus. He's wearing an orange raincoat today. It's seen better days. There's a hole in the hood. A steady stream of the downpour that's blanketed the city this morning is running down the side of his face.

I make a mental note to stop and pick up a new raincoat for him, size medium from the looks of it.

I scrub my hand over my forehead. "I thought I'd stay ahead of the rain on my bike, but it has no mercy."

He glances over at my bike. I leaned it against a tree a few feet back from where we're sitting.

"I didn't expect to see you today." I suck in a deep breath.

The smells of the city change whenever rain lets loose. I wasn't about to waste the opportunity to enjoy that so I put on a pair of shorts, a hooded sweatshirt and hopped on my bike.

"I was up early," he admits. "Sleep doesn't always come easy when your mind pokes around in your past."

Amen.

I didn't catch a wink last night. Watching Katie with another man had my thoughts racing. There's no way in hell I could quiet them enough for sleep to take hold.

"I'm here to listen." I shield my eyes from the rain. "We can take this to a coffee shop a couple of blocks from here. I'll buy you a cup."

"Did I ever tell you how much Lois loved dancing in the rain?"

"I don't think so," I lie. "Did she drag you outside whenever it rained?"

He nods, a smile taking over his mouth. "We'd head up to the roof of our building and dance the storm away."

"Was she a good dancer?"

He leans his head back far enough that raindrops pummel his cheeks. "The best dancer in the world. I'd trade every day I have left for one last dance with her."

My gaze shifts to the river.

"I'll take you up on that coffee if you'll throw in a glazed donut." He taps my shoulder. "You can tell me about what's got you troubled."

"I'm troubled?" I ask with a laugh, even though he hit the nail on the head.

"You've been since the day I met you." He nods. "Whatever her name is, if she's walking this earth, you need to make it right, Gage."

He's right. I do need to make it right with Katie. I plan on doing just that.

Chapter 12

Kate

"We should start praying for rain." Natalie locks the door of the boutique. "We had a blockbuster day."

We did.

Both of our bridal consultants were booked solid today, but we also managed to squeeze in seven walk-in appointments. Natalie took care of three and I handled the rest.

Not every bride-to-be found the dress of her dreams, but we sold several, and our alterations department was busy too.

"Should we order pizza?" Natalie asks as her gaze slides over her phone's screen. "My hubs is working out with his buddies tonight."

"Can I get a rain check?"

"Are you seeing last night's guy again tonight?"

"His name is Preston and no, not tonight."

"Because he wore you out last night?" She smirks.

Hardly. I was a mess after seeing Gage outside the boutique. Preston didn't notice because most of his focus was on his phone. A big deal is set to go down in his office today.

We said goodnight with a chaste kiss on the lips after I finished a glass of white wine.

He wanted to take me home, but I insisted on going alone. I told him I was tired. He didn't argue.

"It wasn't like that."

"What was it like?" She glances out the window at the rain beating down on the city.

"Fine," I answer without much thought.

"Fine?" she parrots back, amusement lacing her tone. "You looked way too good for the evening to turn out fine."

The added emphasis she puts on the last word lures a soft smile to my mouth.

"He had a work issue." I shrug a shoulder. "His eyes were glued to his phone."

"Dump him," she says with a grin as she walks closer to me. "If a man can't turn off his phone when he's with you, he's not a keeper, Kate."

I'd agree, but I've been known to take phone calls from panicked brides when I've been on a date. Preston was as attentive as he could be considering that the client who called him repeatedly last night apparently has him on speed dial.

"Did Gage ever ignore you to talk on his phone?"

My head pops up at the question. She can't know how ironic it is, so I fill in the blanks for her. "No, but he dumped me just a few days before our wedding. No explanation, no apology. He just ended things."

Her hand jumps to cover her mouth. "Oh, shit, Kate. I had no idea."

I tuck a hand in the pocket of my red skirt. "It's not a story I like sharing."

"I understand." Her gaze ducks to the floor. "He's an idiot."

Many people have claimed the same thing over the years. First, it was my parents and my brother. When I moved to New York, it was Tilly and Olivia. Even a couple of the men I've dated have weighed in on Gage when I've shared the story of my biggest heartbreak.

"It was forever ago." I walk toward a rack of veils. "He's a part of my past."

"Who stepped right into the middle of your present," she points out. "What's his story now?"

"His story?" I bounce back her words with a tilt of my head.

"Has he explained why he dumped you?" She locks eyes with me. "You want to know, don't you?"

Ignoring her direct questions, I run my fingers over the veils. "I got over him a long time ago."

I catch the skeptical look in her eyes when I glance back at her.

"I've moved on," I go on, pushing the wheeled rack a few inches toward the corridor that leads to the stockroom. "I'm sure he has to. We're not the same people who almost got married five years ago."

We both jump at the sound of a knock on the door.

It's not the first time a bride has come back after her appointment to purchase a dress she passed over.

When the realization sets in that a woman has walked away from her dream gown, she'll try and right that wrong as soon as possible.

"I'll get it." Natalie walks back to where she was standing just moments ago.

She peers out into the rain, her hand moving over the lock on the door.

"It's Athena."

Athena Millett owns the flower shop next door. She's a beautiful breath of fresh air.

"Come in." Natalie tugs her in by her arm. "What are you doing out in the rain?"

Athena holds out a large bouquet of multi-colored pastel roses. "I'm making a delivery."

I contracted Athena to handle the flowers in the boutique. She sends someone over twice a week to freshen the bouquets that dot the interior of the showroom.

Her beautiful flower arrangements help set the romantic mood of Katie Rose Bridal.

"You could have waited until morning." I look over the cute white pants and checkered white and blue blouse she's wearing. "Why would you risk getting that outfit wet? Those roses are beautiful, by the way. They'll look perfect in the showroom."

She takes a step closer to me, her blue eyes narrowing. "These aren't for the boutique, Kate. These are for you."

I gaze down at the flowers.

"Preston has excellent taste." Natalie grazes her fingertip over the petal of a pale purple rose.

"Preston?" Athena's gaze volleys between Natalie and me. "Who's Preston?"

A knot settles in my stomach as I stare down at the breathtaking bouquet. "The man who sent the flowers?"

Athena's golden brown hair floats over her shoulders as she shakes her head. "You should read the card, Kate. He came in an hour ago and filled it out himself."

"Who came in?" Natalie's lip purse. "Gage Burke?"

Athena gives my hand a gentle squeeze. "He insisted I give them to you before you left for the day."

I pluck the small white envelope from the bouquet she's holding.

Turning my back to her and Natalie, I break the seal on the envelope with my fingernail and slide out the card.

My gaze glides over the handwriting. It's just as I remember it; hurried and crowded, but completely legible to me.

> *Katie,*
> *I'm sorry for scaring you yesterday.*
> *I'm sorry for that day five years ago.*
> *I'm sorry for every day since.*
> *Gage*

"What does it say?" Natalie asks over my shoulder. "Gage sent the flowers, didn't he?"

I nod.

"Are you all right, Kate?" Athena's hand lands in the middle of my back, giving it a soft pat. "I'm sorry if I upset you."

"You didn't," I say in a voice that is too weak to be my own. "I'm fine."

"I can take the flowers and put them…"

"No." I pivot on my heel to face her and Natalie. "I'll take care of the flowers. I know just where to put them."

Chapter 13

Gage

Jesus.

I stare at the doorway of Tin Anchor and the woman who just walked in.

Katie is drenched to the bone. Her blonde hair is a wild wet tangle around her face from the wind and rain. The red skirt she's wearing hugs her every curve and the white blouse clinging to her is see-through, revealing a white lace bra underneath.

She's never been more beautiful than she is at this moment.

Her gaze scans the room until it lands on my face.

Anger pouts her pink lips the way it always has.

She marches toward me, the bouquet of roses I ordered for her, clutched in her fist.

She slams the flowers onto to the top of the bar, scattering wet petals everywhere. Only a few heads turn in our direction. The baseball game on the wide screen TV is the main attraction tonight.

Katie's hazel eyes reach mine in a heated gaze. "What the hell is wrong with you, Gage?"

Years ago, I would have stripped her bare and fucked the rage right out of her.

Katie never went to bed angry. I was between her legs before any of our arguments reached their stride. I'd eat her to orgasm and then she'd ride me, taking whatever she needed from my cock; from me.

Frustration was never the norm for her. It always took something big to push her over the edge from calm and peaceful to fury.

Dammit, I wish I could touch her now, taste her, fuck her.

"I see you got the flowers, Katie."

Her eyes widen. "I don't want flowers from you."

I glance down at the tattered remains of the roses. "Duly noted."

"I don't need flowers from you."

I know. She needs the impossible. She needs me to turn back time to a day five years ago when I ripped her heart from her chest and tore it into a million pieces.

"Tell me what you do need," I tempt fate by putting that out there.

Her top teeth latch onto her bottom lip as she thinks it through.

She's inside my bar. I want her to stay. I don't want her to walk out of here yet.

I step in to give her more time and to keep her in place. "I'll make you a whiskey sour."

"No," her reply is instant. "I don't drink those anymore."

The declaration spears my heart. It's just a drink, but it was our drink. I was the person who introduced her to hard liquor. I poured her a shot of straight whiskey the night we moved in together.

Her throat burned, a tear welled in her eye, and when I leaned forward to brush my lips over hers, I could taste the whiskey on her mouth.

Weeks later, I made myself a whiskey sour, and she sipped it too, stealing kisses from me between swallows.

"What do you drink?" I ask even though I can guess.

When you spend enough time behind a bar, you get a sense for what people crave when they walk in.

The woman across from me now is elegant and sophisticated. She carries herself with an unspoken grace that wasn't there when she was twenty-two-years-old.

A martini. She drinks martinis.

"When I do drink it's usually a dirty martini." Her eyes scan the withering rose petals covering the top of the bar. "I'm leaving."

"Do you have plans?" I have no right to ask her that, but I do.

The thought of her rushing off to see the suit from last night knots my gut. It's not my business, but I haven't been able to shake the image of her holding his hand as they walked down the sidewalk.

"I'm not answering that." She says harshly, her arms crossing her chest.

"Are you seeing him again?" I push for more because I want her to tell me that he's nobody.

Her bare ring finger gives me hope, but it doesn't mean that she's not in love with the guy.

"Who?" she spits the word at me.

"The guy you met up with last night."

Her eyes narrow. "Preston."

I don't want to know his goddamn name. That only adds to the hell I've put myself in.

"Preston," I repeat it back in a low voice. "Is Preston your boyfriend?"

Her fingers skim over the top button on her blouse. "He's a man I've been seeing."

The heavens must be smiling down on me tonight. He's not her boyfriend. She would have confirmed that. It's a casual thing.

I take that as a sign and jump in with both feet. "I want to talk, Katie. I want to explain what happened five years ago."

Her gaze darts to the shelves on the wall behind me. I watch her face intently as she scans each of them. I see the moment when realization hits her.

Memories of the life we shared back in California are on one of those shelves. I've never let them go. I've carried them with me everywhere.

Chapter 14

Kate

My gaze catches on the wall behind the bar.

A large mirror hangs in the center, but the glass shelves that border it are crowded with liquor bottles.

My eyes lock on a leather-scented candle, a collection of poetry books, and a chess set on the top shelf.

I take in each item. All are a memory of my past. The past I shared with Gage.

My heart feels like it's squeezing into a tight ball inside my chest.

I tap my hand over it, willing it to stop aching.

"Do you want me to clean these flowers up, Gage?" A deep voice asks.

I turn and look into the face of a dark-haired man wearing glasses. He shoves his hand in my direction. "I'm Zeke."

His arms are covered with tattoos. He's wearing a black T-shirt with *Tin Anchor* printed across the front in white lettering.

I take his hand for a soft shake, not offering anything but a half-smile.

Gage slides a glass of water toward me. "This is Katie."

Zeke's eyes widen. "I've heard about you."

I'm tempted to ask what he's heard, but I stop myself. I don't care what Gage has told him about me because I doubt like hell he included the part where he dumped me days before our wedding so he could sail the high seas.

"I'll take care of the flowers," Gage pats Zeke's forearm. "I'd appreciate if you take over the bar. Callie's got the floor covered."

"No problem," Zeke says with a smile. "It was good to meet you, Katie."

"Kate," I correct him. "I prefer Kate."

"Kate it is." Zeke nods before he turns his attention to a man at the end of the bar waving his hand in the air.

Gage crosses his arms over his chest. He's not wearing a Tin Anchor shirt. He's dressed in a black sweater and dark jeans.

His jaw is peppered with a five o'clock shadow.

I may not want to admit it, but he's still the most handsome man I've ever seen.

"I wish I could turn the clock back, Katie." His green eyes lock on my face. "I'd give anything to make that happen."

"You can't." I push the glass of water back at him. I don't want anything from this man, especially a trip down memory lane.

"You deserved better," he admits on a low sigh. "I regret the way I handled things."

"You regret the way you handled things?" I question back.

That's a hell of a lot different than regretting breaking my heart.

"I do." He scrubs his hand over the back of his neck. "I panicked and took off."

Panicked because you realized that you didn't love me and that meant you couldn't marry me.

I've suspected as much since the day he broke off our engagement. Why else does a man leave a woman right before he's supposed to marry her?

My family and friends back in California all tried to convince me it wasn't about me. They twisted the situation into something it wasn't by assuring me that he left because of his immaturity or the fear born from loving me too much.

If Gage loved me as much as he said he did, he would have been standing at the end of the aisle waiting to exchange vows with me.

"We don't need to do this." I take a step away from the bar. "It's history now. Why it happened doesn't matter anymore."

"It matters." He runs his hands through his hair.

It's shorter now than it was back then. I used to tug on the back of it when his face was between my thighs.

Gage's mouth took me places that I haven't been since. His cock made the journey even more unforgettable.

I've had a handful of lovers since I moved to Manhattan, but there's nothing about any of them that I can remember.

My gaze stalls on his left wrist.

I blink twice to be sure I'm not seeing things.

He's wearing the bracelet.

I made that bracelet for his twenty-third birthday. I bought the stone beads from a craft supply store and looped them together with fishing line I found in the garage at my parents' place.

He told me he loved it when he opened it. He swore he'd never take it off his wrist.

I rub at my forehead. Emotion is clouding my vision.

"I need to go," I whisper into the air around me.

I can't breathe. None of this makes any sense. He left me. Why the hell is he still holding onto things that symbolize the love we once shared?

"Katie, please," he pleads in a low tone. "I want to talk to you."

I stare at him, unable to form any words.

He fills the silence. "Fate put us in the same place for a reason."

Fate. It's Gage's answer to everything. He used to tell me that fate put me in his path the afternoon we met on the campus at UCLA.

I was there to earn a business degree. Gage's future was in medicine.

"You are my true north," he lowers his voice. "I was meant to walk into your store the other day. Our story isn't over."

My heart clouds with a dozen conflicting emotions. My knees shake. My ears ring.

I can't do this.

"Our story is over," I whisper back.

"Not according to fate."

I almost laugh at his choice of words. "You waited for fate to find me. All of this time, you never once bothered to look for me."

He shakes his head, his hand flying into the air between us to stop me from continuing. "Katie, I…"

"Go to hell," I interrupt him. "Take fate with you."

Chapter 15

Kate

Gage calls after me as I march out of Tin Anchor.

I look up and down the sidewalk, trying to decide where to go.

I should go home, but I don't want to be alone. My heart feels like it's been flipped inside out.

"Katie, wait."

I glance over my shoulder to see Gage standing at the entrance to his bar with a denim jacket in his hands.

"Put this on." He moves to drape it over my shoulders. "You're getting wet."

I slap the jacket away with my hands. "I don't need that."

He ignores my protest and slides it over me, tugging the front together. "You should wear it home. You used to catch a cold whenever you got stuck in a rainstorm."

I gaze down at the wet sidewalk. "Don't do that. You can't keep bringing up the past."

"I need to."

His words are bold and direct. There's no hesitation in them at all.

I look up into his green eyes. I used to stare into them for hours, fascinated by the way they seemed to change hue depending on the light in the room.

They are still the most beautiful eyes I've ever seen.

"I don't want you to." I take a step back from him. "We've both moved on. Why bring up the past at this point?"

"You've moved on?" He questions with a lift of his left brow. "With Preston? I thought you said it was casual."

"Not with Preston," I say tightly. "Not with anyone. I meant that I put my life back together. What happened between us was so long ago."

"It feels like yesterday to me." His tone is deep and soothing, just as it was years ago when I needed reassurance about the problems that would pop up in my life.

Gage was always the voice of reason. He could help me see the light at the end of the tunnel, regardless if there was one or not.

"Give me a chance to explain what happened, Katie."

Taking a step toward the street, the rain beats down on me. I tug the jacket closer to my body. It's a reminder of forever ago when Gage would offer his jacket to me whenever I was cold.

Gage follows my lead, taking the spot next to me as I scan the oncoming traffic for an available taxi.

"Come back inside," he insists. "You don't have to talk to me. You can have a coffee and sit at a table by yourself. You need to get out of this storm."

I turn to face him, angry that we're standing together in the rain just as we were the day after we met.

Maybe fate does have a hand in what's happening.

"You don't know what I need." I push a finger into his chest. "You don't know me anymore."

Tears bubble up inside of me. I push them back with a heavy swallow and a reminder that I promised myself when I left the boutique with the flowers in my hand that I wouldn't let him see me cry.

"I know you need answers." His gaze glides over my face.

"I don't." I shake my head, trying to add weight to the lie that just left my lips.

His hand jumps to my chin. "You do."

I don't pull back from his touch because I've craved it for years. I stare into his eyes. "There's nothing you can say to me that will change a thing. You don't understand what you did to me."

His eyes drop to the front of the jacket. "I broke your heart."

I push his hand from my face. "You broke all of me. I couldn't make sense of the world anymore. Everything I knew and believed was turned upside down."

I'm giving him too much. I'm letting him see the most vulnerable parts of me, and that's not what I want.

I have to protect myself at all costs. I have to protect the woman I am now and that broken girl he left behind with a wedding dress in her closet and a heart full of dreams.

"I'm sorry, Katie." His voice is rough and edged with sadness. "I'm so sorry for what I put you through."

Something inside of me cracks. Hearing the words and seeing the emotion swimming in those green eyes shatters me.

My hand covers my lips as I let out a sob.

"I need to explain." He inches even closer to me. "Please let me explain why I left."

I can't hear him tell me that he doubted his love. I've known it for years, but I can't bear to hear the words leave his lips. "No. It doesn't matter anymore."

"It matters." His hands fist at his sides. "All of it matters."

"You stopped loving me," I say the words to give them a voice; my voice.

A confirmation nod from him won't split me in two the same way his words will.

"Never." He exhales harshly. "I never stopped loving you."

I never stopped loving you either.

I stare into his eyes as I hold tight to the words, not saying a thing.

I can't still love him, can I?

"Katie," he pauses, his hands jumping to my cheeks as the rain falls on us. "The day I left... that morning, I found out...Katie, I found out I had a daughter."

Chapter 16

Gage

Katie's mouth drops open. She stumbles back on her feet, but my hands are wrapped around her forearms before her knees give out.

I've pictured this moment for years. I've rehearsed how I would tell her about my daughter. I had the build-up all worked out.

In my fucked-up optimistic mind, we'd be having a drink or dinner, and I'd open up to her slowly.

She'd be naturally shocked, but in time understanding would replace that.

Thunder claps above us as her eyes seek out mine. I see the plea in them. It's the same plea that was there the day I told her I couldn't marry her.

Back then, I couldn't find the words to tell her that I had a child.

"What?" she asks, staring at me like I've grown a second head. Confusion doesn't even begin to describe her expression.

"I'll explain all of it." I look up when another blast of thunder echoes over Manhattan. "Let's go back inside."

Her gaze darts to the windows of Tin Anchor. People have been ducking inside in a steady stream to escape the rain. It's more crowded now than when we left a few minutes ago.

"I can't go back inside." Her arms shake beneath my touch. "I can't think in there."

"There's a coffee shop around the corner," I suggest because I can't let her walk away without the full story.

You don't throw something like this at someone without a foundation of understanding.

"I should go home." She tries to tug her arms free. "I have to think."

"I have to explain," I counter. "We can get a coffee and talk."

Her gaze drops with a shake of her head. "I can't be around people right now."

The office in the back of my bar is private and secluded, but it's uncomfortable. I'm not going to talk to Katie about why I left her while we're sitting in two folding metal chairs with an old air conditioner unit humming noisily beside us.

"We can go to my apartment," I suggest knowing that it's a ridiculous idea. "I live three blocks from here."

Studying my face, her brows pinch together. "Your apartment?"

I tighten my grip on her arms out of fear that she'll bolt if I let go. "Just to talk. I'll make us coffee. I'll explain about Kristin."

Her bottom lip trembles. "Kristin?"

Fuck. Just fuck.

I'm throwing too much at her at once, and there's no place for her to hide. She bats her long eyelashes as the rain showers her face.

"My daughter," I clarify. "Kristin."

"That's a pretty name," she whispers. "Is she pretty?"

I see her resolve break right before me. Tears stream down her face with the raindrops, melding together before they fall from her chin.

Children were never part of our plan. Katie was insistent that we would remain as a family of two for eternity.

I questioned it when I felt the longing that a man does to have a child after he meets the woman he's destined to love.

She'd overheard her mom one too many times complaining about the life that she might have had, the career, and travel dreams that were snuffed out by the positive sign on a pregnancy test.

Katie wanted her career and me. I wanted her. I was willing to sacrifice fatherhood for her until I discovered that I was already a dad to a beautiful little girl.

"Let's go to my place to talk," I suggest again because I need to get her out of the rain and I need time to formulate what I'll say. "We'll be alone there."

She nods without a word.

I glance to the side and catch sight of a couple exiting a taxi.

I glide my right hand down Katie's arm until it catches her wrist. I tug her toward the car. "Get in, Katie."

She slides onto the torn leather backseat, her gaze trained on the rain out the window.

I sit next to her, tell the driver where to drop us off, and pray that I'll be able to put the pieces of this beautiful woman's heart back together again.

Chapter 17

Kate

A daughter.

Never in the days, months or years of the tortured hell I've put myself in have I imagined that Gage left me because he had a daughter.

He's a father.

"Can I make you a cup of coffee or tea?" Gage glances over his shoulder at me as he unlocks the door to his apartment. "Do you still like Earl Grey with steamed milk?"

I only liked it back then because he was intent on me drinking it one chilly Christmas Eve.

His grandmother had lived on the brand of tea that Gage bought when he went to the grocery store to get the fixings for an extravagant holiday dinner for us.

He came back with the tea, a loaf of day-old bread, and a can of chicken noodle soup.

His wallet was on the kitchen counter, so some coins and a few dollar bills in the pocket of his torn jeans were the only currency he had to pay for our festive feast.

It was the most delicious meal I've ever had.

"I don't need anything to drink," I whisper as I follow him into his home.

His home.

The only home Gage had before we met was a bedroom on the second floor of his parents' lavish estate in the Hollywood Hills.

"I'll get you a blanket." He heads down a hallway. The sweater on his back is yanked over his head just as he disappears into a room.

I glance around, taking in the space that he lives in.

It's nothing like the apartment we shared in California. This one has an open living room and kitchen with white walls. The floors are a light hardwood with mismatched throw rugs under the sofa and two leather chairs. A rectangular cherry wood coffee table is far enough from the sofa that Gage can rest his feet on it when he's watching TV, just as he always did back when I'd cuddle up next to him and stare at the screen.

I look to the right where a square dining room table sits near a window that faces the neighboring building.

The long black curtains on the window are pushed to the side, affording me a perfect view of the rain hitting the glass.

I scrub my hand over my forehead. My hair is plastered to my head. My makeup must be a mess on my face, and yet I don't care.

I'm in shock.

I'm sure my heart stopped beating outside of Tin Anchor when Gage told me that he has a daughter.

I scan the room for a picture of her, but I come up empty.

There's no artwork or personal items. There's nothing in here that captures who Gage is except for the light blue knitted blanket hanging over the arm of the black leather sofa.

I walk over to it, studying the wool that has now loosened. I worked on it for weeks before I gave it to him on that Christmas Eve when we ate soup and drank tea and made love in our bed.

It was our last holiday together.

The pad of his bare feet on the floor draws my gaze back to the hallway.

He's dressed in a black T-shirt and the same jeans he had on earlier. His shoes and socks are gone. A white fluffy blanket is in his hands.

"I have clothes you can change into," he offers as he shoves the blanket at me. "I put a pair of sweatpants and a T-shirt in the bathroom for you. I have a dryer. I can dry your skirt and blouse."

I look down at my wet clothes and the denim jacket that's still draped over me. I place the blanket on the sofa so I can slide the jacket off.

The sight of my bra under my blouse flushes my cheeks in embarrassment.

Gage has seen me naked, laid bare and wanting. He's aware of the freckle below my right breast and the mole that sits just above my hipbone. He used to trace a fingertip over the scar on my left knee. It's a constant reminder of the surgery I had after a failed landing during a gymnastics class when I was fifteen.

His tender touch always made me feel less self-conscious about it.

I toss the jacket at him and pick up the blanket, wrapping it around me to shield my lingerie from his gaze.

"This is fine," I say, my voice still quaking. "I can't stay long."

I shouldn't be here at all.

That's what I should be saying to him, but I let him bring me here because I was in a daze. I was lost the moment he told me that he has a child.

That was something I told him I'd never give him.

Someone else did.

"I'll make some coffee," he says, draping the jacket over the back of a chair. He takes a step toward the kitchen before I stop him with a question.

"How old is she?" Tears form in the corners of my eyes.

I tried to convince myself on the taxi ride here that she wasn't conceived when we were together. If he cheated on me and the result is a beautiful little girl, how can I feel rage at that?

How can I not?

"Nine," he answers with a soft smile. "My little angel is nine-years-old."

Chapter 18

Gage

I could see the curiosity in her tear-filled eyes before she asked the question. I knew that as soon as Katie found out about my daughter, that she'd wonder if I cheated on her.

If she only knew that my heart, my soul and yes, my body has only ever belonged to her.

I watch as she taps her thumb against each of the fingers on her right hand. She's silently counting out the years, trying to determine how old I was when Kristin was born.

Scratching the side of my nose, I fill in the blanks. "When I met Kristin she was four. She was born a few days after my twentieth birthday."

"Four?" she questions back with a genuine look of surprise on her face. "You didn't know about her before then?"

"Not until the day I…"

My voice drifts because I should say, "*not until the day I fucking broke your heart.*"

"Until the day you left," she says softly. "You said earlier that you found out that morning. How?"

"Her mother called me."

Katie's eyes narrow. "Her mother? Who is her mother?"

I know the name I'm about to say is going to sting Katie. I only had one semi-serious girlfriend before we met.

Madison Velmont was a constant in my life when I was growing up. Her mom took care of the cleaning and cooking needs of my family. She was a single woman trying to support a daughter on her own.

They lived in an apartment in downtown Los Angeles but spent every day at my parents' estate until seven p.m. when they'd catch a bus that would take them home.

When it came time for Madison's prom, my mom insisted that I take her.

I didn't complain. She was a cute brunette who was always flirting with me.

A year after I was accepted into UCLA, Madison got a full academic scholarship to Vanderbilt University.

She wanted me to make the move to Nashville with her. I refused. She said she loved me. I told her the feeling wasn't mutual and she took off without another word.

Our paths didn't cross again until she made a trip back to California to settle her mother's modest estate.

That's when she called me and dropped the bombshell that eight months after we broke up, Kristin was born.

"Is it Madison?" Katie blurts out. "Madison is her mom, isn't she?"

Katie was a virgin when we met. I wasn't by a long shot. Madison wasn't the only lover I had, but she was the one my parents mentioned one night when they had too much wine over dinner.

"*I always thought you'd end up with Madison*," my dad slurred.

"*It's a shame you didn't*," my mom added after her goddamn fiftieth sip of the expensive Chardonnay they dug out of their wine cellar to toast to my engagement to Katie.

I'll never forget the look on my fiancée's face or the tears that streamed down her cheeks on our ride home.

I scolded my parents for that. I threatened to cut them from my life if they ever uttered Madison's name again.

They didn't until the day I told them that they were grandparents.

"Yes, Madison is Kristin's mother," I answer.

Silence stretches between us as she studies my face. "You left me to be with her…with them. You went to be with them, didn't you?"
I did, and I didn't.

I consider my next words carefully. "I couldn't be around anyone when I first found out, so I got on my dad's sailboat the day after I talked to you. I was gone for a week… maybe ten days. When I got back, I took a trip to Nashville to meet Kristin."

I don't mention that my first stop after I hit dry land was the apartment we shared, but Katie wasn't there.

She broke the lease and cleared her stuff out. I picked up what was left from the landlord and stored it at my parents' house until I settled into my own place in Nashville. I unpacked it then. I've kept those items close to me ever since.

A shaky breath leaves her. "Did you marry Madison?"

My reply is quick and clear. "No."

The only reaction from her is a blink of her eyes.

"I went to Nashville to meet my daughter," I go on, "I stayed because I had to."

I pat the middle of my chest so she understands that love kept me in Nashville. The love I felt for my daughter the moment I met her only grew as time passed.

"So, Madison, Kristin, and you all live here now?" She gazes down the hallway. "Will they be back soon? I don't want to be here when they come back."

"I've never lived with Madison," I stress each word. "I lived in the same apartment building as her and Kristin in Nashville, but we were never together, Katie."

"Oh." Her eyes widen. "I just assumed that you moved in with them."

"No," I shake my head. "We co-parented until…"

"Until what?" She takes a step closer, the blanket around her shoulders sliding down.

"Madison got married a year-and-a-half ago." My hands fist at my sides. "Her husband landed a job in London. They made the move eight months ago."

"London as in across the ocean?" She questions with narrowed eyes. "How does that work? Does Kristin come here for vacations or something?"

"Something," I mutter.

It's too fucked up to get into right now. The entire situation is a goddamn nightmare that I don't think I'll ever wake up from.

Her gaze drops to the floor. "This is a lot to take in."

She doesn't even know the half of it yet. My life since I left her has been out of control. I haven't felt centered until this minute.

Katie always made me feel that everything would be all right.

"I'm going to go now." She tugs her phone out of the pocket of her skirt.

Her fingers fly over the screen. She hesitates before she types again. It's obvious that she's exchanging messages with someone. I hope to hell it's not Preston.

"Can we talk again soon?" I ask because I need to tell her more. I want to explain everything to her.

"Maybe." She sighs. "My friend is sending a car for me so I should get downstairs."

"Your friend?"

She nods but doesn't offer anything else.

A mental image of her finding comfort in Preston's arms and his bed flashes before me. I push it aside because my petty jealousy doesn't compare to what she's feeling.

"I'll walk you down," I offer.

"No." Her hand darts in the air to stop me. "I can find my own way out."

I take a step toward her, but it only results in a step backward for her.

"Thank you, Katie," I say hoarsely. "Thank you for coming and for listening."

The only response from her is a brisk nod before she's out my apartment door.

Chapter 19

Kate

"Are you sure this isn't a bother?" I ask him as I stare at his profile.

Sebastian Wolf turns to look at me, his blue eyes scanning my face. "I just finished a training exercise with a handful of rookies. I was on my way to headquarters to drop off the car when Matilda called and said you were in trouble."

I'm grateful that Tilly called him.

He shifts his gaze back to the road as he goes on, "I almost came racing down here with my gun drawn."

"When Tilly said she was sending a car, I had no idea it was a police car." I manage a soft laugh. "I left my store without my purse."

"How did you get to Greenwich Village?" He stops the sedan at a red light.

"When I got to the subway I realized I didn't have my MetroCard, or my wallet, or my keys." I rest my head against the headrest.

"Are you a jumper?" He laughs. "Tell me you didn't jump the turnstile and ride for free."

"In this skirt?" I smooth my hands over my lap.

"You busked for change? I've heard you sing at karaoke, Kate. It must have taken hours for you to make fare with that voice."

I laugh at his repeated jokes. I know he's trying to cheer me up. The text message I sent to Tilly was ominous.

I told her I was falling apart and needed her.

She replied that I had to get in a taxi and head out to her house in Queens.

That's when I responded that I didn't have my wallet or my keys.

"I gave Natalie money to get us coffee this afternoon. When she came back to the store, I shoved the change in my pocket. It was just enough."

"It's your lucky day."

I shake my head. "I wouldn't say that."

My phone chimes. I glance down at the text message from Natalie in response to the one I just sent to her asking if I can stop by her apartment to pick up her set of keys to the boutique so I can get my things.

Natalie: *I'm still at work. I'm getting a head start on inventory.*

"Good news?" he asks as he drives through an intersection.

"Very good news." I breathe a small sigh of relief. At least something is falling into place for me tonight. "Can you take me to my store?"

"On one condition." He flicks on the right turn signal.

"What's that?"

"Let Matilda take care of you tonight." He flashes me a smile. "My wife is worried about you. I don't know what you're dealing with, Kate, but we're both here for you. Have dinner with us. I'll do the cooking."

"You two are the best."

"Matilda is the best." He sighs. "I have no idea what I did in my past life to deserve that woman."

I stare out the window as we drive through the city. He doesn't push for more conversation. Sebastian knows instinctively when to give someone time with his or her thoughts.

Once he pulls up to the boutique, I unbuckle my seatbelt. "I'll be back in a minute."

"This is a no parking zone so make it quick." He chuckles.

I step out of the car and glance down at the blue NYPD logo on the side. "I think you'll be all right."

***

"Dinner was delicious, Sebastian." I place my linen napkin on the table next to my empty plate.

There are always two things I can count on when I come to Tilly and Sebastian's home for dinner. Good food is never in shortage and there are plenty of hugs.

Sebastian got a big one when we stepped in the door after taking a taxi from Manhattan to Queens. After we dropped off the police car, Sebastian grabbed an umbrella from his office and we set out toward the subway stop that is nearest police headquarters.

He spotted a taxi and since the rain had picked up again, he told me the ride was his treat. It didn't take long until the driver was parked in front of the house in Queens where Tilly, Sebastian and their dog, Lunar, live.

Lunar lunged at us when Sebastian unlocked the door. Tilly ran to her husband, launching herself in his arms and diving her fingers into his black hair.

After they kissed and whispered something to each other, she pulled me into a tight embrace.

It was the first time I felt truly comfortable in hours.

"I'm going to take Lunar for a walk." Sebastian pushes back from the table. "If you need anything, I'll have my phone with me."

He leans down to kiss Tilly softly on the lips.

I stare at her face as she watches him walk to the front door before he pushes it open after grabbing Lunar's leash and the umbrella he brought home from his office.

The slam of the door behind him breaks the spell she's under. She turns to look at me.

"I love him a little more each day," she confesses. "He's worried about you, Kate. I am too."

I know that it's because of the text messages I sent her earlier.

I told her that my ex-fiancé had dropped a bombshell on me and I needed her.

I wasn't surprised that she leapt into action after I told her that I was stuck in Greenwich Village with only my cell phone.

"What happened?" she asks, tilting her head.

She's wearing one of Sebastian's T-shirts and a pair of denim overalls. Her face is freshly washed. She looks like she's twenty-years-old, even though she's only a year younger than me.

I take a sip of the water I've been drinking throughout dinner.

"Is it too hard to talk about?" Her hand inches across the table to cover mine. "We can talk about work or watch a movie. I'm going to paint the extra bedroom this weekend. If you want we can start on that tonight."

Active hands quiet a busy mind.

My mom would say that to me daily after Gage left. Tilly follows that advice when she has too much to think about.

"You finally decided on a color?" I ask with a smile.

Ever since Tilly and Sebastian bought this house and moved in, they've spent a lot of their free time working to make it their own.

It's quaint and charming with a brick fireplace in the corner of the living room and a kitchen with white cabinets and gray granite countertops. It's a mesh of both of their styles.

"Yellow." She sighs. "We picked it together. We're going to make it into a guest bedroom for when my folks come to visit."

"I'll come back on the weekend to help you paint," I offer.

Her blue eyes scan my face. "I'm worried about you."

I squeeze her hand before I slide mine onto my lap. "He has a daughter."

She sits back in her chair. "Gage has a daughter?"

"Kristin," I say her name. "She's nine. Kristin is nine."

"Nine?" Her brow furrows. "She was born before you two met?"

I nod. "He didn't know about her until the day he broke up with me."

She shoves a hand through her hair. "Wow. This is just...wow, Kate."

My gaze travels past her shoulder to a framed picture of her and Sebastian on their wedding day.

Regret bites at me. I didn't get to have that with Gage. I now know why but it doesn't change what I felt back in those moments. I had to tell my parents, and the three hundred guests who had RSVP'd that there wasn't going to be a celebration of the love that Gage and I shared.

"Is he married to the little girl's mom?"

I turn my attention back to my best friend. "No. She lives in London with her husband and Kristin."

Tilly pinches her bottom lip. "He told you all of this tonight?"

"He sent flowers to the store. I went to throw them in his face, but then he told me about his daughter."

She inches the wooden chair she's sitting in closer to me. "You must be in shock. I can't imagine what you're feeling right now."

"Numb," I say with a heave of my shoulders.

I don't add that a small part of me feels relief; relief that I finally know what took Gage away from me days before we were set to say our *I do's*.

Chapter 20

Gage

Staying home wasn't an option after Katie left my apartment last night. I needed a distraction, so I slipped on a pair of shoes, grabbed an umbrella and took the stairs as soon as I heard the elevator doors close. I reached the lobby just in time to see her getting into the front seat of a police car.

It took off down the street. I hit the sidewalk to walk back to Tin Anchor.

By the time I got there, the place was packed so I jumped behind the bar to help Zeke. I served drinks and talked people through their problems until closing time.

When I got home, I dropped into bed, but sleep didn't come for another hour or two.

I was restless. I couldn't shake the look on Katie's face when I told her about Kristin.

The ball is in her court now. Whether she volleys it back to me is completely up to her.

"You're here earlier than usual." Gus walks up behind me. "This brilliant blue sky was hiding behind those rain clouds."

I look up at the rising sun. "It was worth it."

"Storms are always worth it." He brushes past me to sit on the bench. "Lois used to say that the darkest skies give way to the brightest days."

"She was a smart woman."

"You're telling me?" He laughs causing the skin at the corner of his eyes to crease. "Why do you think I married her?"

Because you loved her. Because you had faith in her love for you.

I lacked that with Katie. It took me months to realize that. I didn't give her a chance to respond to the news that I was a dad. I stole that from her by making a life-changing decision on my own.

I was a twenty-four-year-old fool who saw the world through a black and white lens.

Katie didn't want kids. I suddenly had one.

In my mind those two things couldn't add up to a happy ending, so I did what I thought was best at the time.

Gus glances at the tree behind us. "You're on foot today?"

I tug at the waistband of my black running shorts. I'm shirtless. My phone is strapped to my bicep so I can listen to my favorite playlist as I run through the streets of Manhattan.

It's an escape at the beginning of my day. The bar fills that need at the end of the day. It's the hours in between that are the hardest.

"I get a better workout on foot." I laugh. "I have to work off that donut I had for breakfast."

"When the weather turns we should do this at the coffee shop." Gus looks down at his watch. "I think that'll be sometime around December, January if we're lucky."

"We'll make it happen."

He doesn't show up every day, but I know that my presence brings him a sense of peace. I haven't pried, but I sense that Gus is traveling through the latter part of his life completely alone.

"You've lost weight." He wiggles the fingers of his right hand at me.

I pat my abs. "I'm holding steady."

He shakes his head. "Some of that weight that's been on your shoulders is gone."

He couldn't have spoken truer words this morning.

I may not know where I stand with Katie, but I woke up feeling lighter for the first time in five years.

"Confessions will do that to a man, Gus."

His graying brows pop up. "Amen."

I stare out at the East River. The only sounds around us are the traffic helicopters overheard and the light wind whipping from the north.

"What's her name, Gage?"

I look down at him. "Katie."

"Does Katie know what she has in you?"

A coward who couldn't face his own truth five years ago?

I stretch my right arm over my head. "I know that there isn't another woman on this earth like her."

"She's your Lois, is she?"

I smile at that. It's a bar set high in his eyes, so I answer honestly. "She's my Lois. She's always been and will always be my Lois."

***

"Does Kristin look like you?"

My head lifts. After my confession last night, I prayed I would hear that sweet voice again, but I had no idea it would be this soon.

I watch as Katie settles onto a barstool. She looks incredible. Her long blonde hair is straight. Her makeup is slightly bolder than it's been since I walked back into her life. She's wearing jeans and a red blouse that's tied at the waist.

A few men in the bar turn to look at her. It sparks envy deep within me.

They aren't carrying around the burden of my past mistakes with her.

I can't offer her a clean slate like any of them can, but I can offer her memories of two college kids desperately in love.

I tug my phone out of the back pocket of my jeans. I scroll through the image library until I land on the most recent picture of my daughter that I have.

I flip the phone around to show Katie the brown-haired, green-eyed ray of sunshine that I love with all of my heart.

"This is Kristin."

Katie leans forward. Her eyes skim the screen. "She's beautiful."

I turn the phone back to face me. The picture was taken at a playground. Kristin had just gotten off a swing. Her hair was bobbing around her shoulders. Her cheeks were flushed pink. The grin on her face was wide, revealing a missing bottom tooth.

It's pure joy in the form of a photograph.

Katie studies my face. "What's she like?"

Staring into her eyes, I rest both of my forearms on the top of the bar. "Smart as a whip, kind, impetuous. She's not afraid to speak her mind."

She breaks eye contact with me with a quick glance at a man sitting two stools away from her.

I straighten. "I'll make you a dirty martini."

"With two olives," she says, smiling enough to part her lips.

I set to work making her drink with a flicker of hope that I haven't felt in years.

Chapter 21

Kate

I sense Gage's gaze on me as I check my phone yet again.

Since he made me a martini, he's been busy tending to the needs of the people sitting at the bar. He seems to know most of them by their first names and their preferred drinks.

He's chatted up both men and women, smiling at them while he prepares what they order.

He's a natural at this. I know he worked behind the bar at a club in Hollywood a few months before we met, but I thought that was for pocket money.

I had no idea that less than a decade later he'd own a bar on the east coast.

I look down at my phone when it chimes.

Preston: *Dinner tomorrow night?*

We've been texting back and forth all day. It was mostly generic messages about the weather and his schedule at work.

He landed a big deal yesterday, so he's in the mood to celebrate.

I glance over to where Gage is talking to a petite brunette woman. I can see the flush of pink on her cheeks as she leans over the bar to showcase the top of her breasts.

Her black dress is low cut and tight.

I don't want jealousy to nip at me but it does. Too much has happened between us for me to care if he's flirting with someone else.

I shouldn't feel anything for him.

I hate that I still do.

Even though I now know that he left because he found out he had a four-year-old daughter, it doesn't change the fact that he never reached out to me after that day.

Once the dust had settled, he could have found me to explain what happened.

I may have changed my number soon after I moved to New York City, but Gage had my parents' phone numbers and my brother's.

My twisted sense of pride kept me from calling him. I promised myself that I wouldn't be the woman who chases a man after he dumps her.

Another message lights up my phone.

Preston: *Or we can meet for a drink tonight. I'm free all night.*

I type back a quick response.

Kate: *I'm having a martini now and one is my limit.*

Preston: *Tell me where and I'll join you.*

"I'm sorry I was pulled away." Gage approaches, glancing at the phone in my hands. "Zeke is on his way in, so I can leave in about fifteen minutes. We can go back to my apartment to talk if you'd like."

I don't want to make that a habit.

There are so many things that I've always imagined saying to Gage if I saw him again. Most start with the "f" word and end with my middle finger in the air pointed in his direction.

Finding out about Kristin may have taken the edge off of some of my anger, but I still feel emotionally spent. Seeing her face makes everything that much more real.

Gage is a father. It's going to take some time to digest that fact.

"I don't think that's a good idea," I say, turning the screen of my phone to shield it from his view.

I'm not sure trudging through more of our past will make any difference to his future or mine.

"Why not?" His gaze darts back to the brunette standing at the end of the bar. She's still laser focused on him. "It's not about her, is it? I don't know her, Katie. She's just a customer."

"I don't care who she is." I sigh heavily. "Who you talk to is none of my business. I'm leaving because I have other plans."

He rakes me over. "A date?"

The tone of his voice is deeper. His jaw has tightened.

"That's none of *your* business," I spit back, emphasizing the word *your*. "I only came here to ask about your daughter. I don't know why I stayed."

I think I do know why.

I want the pain I've been carrying with me for the past five years to go away. It may have lessened its grip on me slightly now that I know that a child was involved, but it doesn't clean the slate.

"You stayed because you feel what I feel."

"What you feel?" I question back.

"You know what I'm talking about." His piercing green eyes lock on my face.

I shrug both shoulders. There's no way in hell I'll confess to feeling anything but anger for him. "I don't."

"What do you feel when you look at me?" He crosses his arms over his chest. I don't know if he's doing it to show off his impressive biceps under the black Tin Anchor T-shirt he's wearing or if it's a defensive stance.

I scrub my hand over my forehead. "You don't want to know."

"I do." He exhales harshly. "Tell me what you feel."

I tilt forward on the bar stool so I can lower my voice to barely more than a whisper. "I'm pissed that you left me and never bothered looking back. You made me feel like shit, Gage."

He takes a step back as if my words slapped him across the face.

"Katie," he whispers, searching my face with his gaze. "I thought you came here to…"

"To what?" I interrupt him. "You thought I came because all is forgiven? I came because I wanted to see the face of your little girl. I came because I want to put all of this to rest. I came because I need this to be over for once and for all so I can go on with my life."

I slide off the barstool. "We can't pretend that the past didn't happen. It did."

"We can sort through it." He rests both his palms on the bar. "We'll sort through it together."

"I've spent five years sorting through it." I pick up my clutch purse. "I moved across the country, made new friends, kissed a few men and learned how to love myself again."

I don't give him a chance to respond. I slip through the crowd of people inside the bar and duck out the door.

Once I'm outside I draw a deep breath into my lungs and type out a message to Preston.

Kate: *I'll meet you at Easton Pub in twenty minutes.*

Chapter 22

Kate

I bounce Arleth on my knee while Olivia looks at a vintage satin wedding gown.

"You're already married, Liv," I point out. "I can put that on hold for Arleth's wedding, but I'll tell you what I tell every mother-of-the-bride who comes into the store. Let your daughter have the last say on her dress."

She glances over her shoulder at me, her tongue sticking out. "Ha! I stopped by Liore today. They're gearing up for a bridal lingerie shoot. I happen to be on a mission to find the perfect dress for the model to wear."

"You're on maternity leave." I laugh. "Shouldn't someone else in your office be on the look-out for the perfect dress?"

"I told them they needed to come here to find a wedding gown." She tosses me a wink. "I want you to have the sale."

"Thank you," I mouth back silently as Arleth settles into my arms.

"If you rock her a bit she might fall asleep."

I look down into the face of Olivia's daughter. I was at the hospital the night she was born. I waited anxiously in the waiting room with Alexander's sister until he came out to announce that Arleth had arrived.

He had tears in his eyes and the widest grin on his mouth.

Gage never got to experience that. He didn't know about his daughter until she was walking and talking.

Precious moments were stolen from him.

Olivia turns to face me. "Have you talked to Gage since you found out about his daughter?"

I called Olivia the other night after I got home from Tilly's house. I didn't want her to hear about it from anyone but me. She understood how confused I was. She told me to take some time to absorb the news and that she was always around if I needed her.

I needed her today, so I texted her and asked her to come by the boutique.

"I saw him last night," I whisper, not wanting to wake Arleth.

The store closed thirty minutes ago. We planned to go to dinner, but take-out may be a better option since I could spend the entire night cradling this sleeping baby in my arms.

"What happened?" Her hands dive into the pockets of the red jumpsuit she's wearing.

"I went to Tin Anchor." I shake my head. "I thought it would help in some way if I saw a picture of his daughter."

"You were curious," she states. "You wanted to put a face to the name. You wanted to see Gage's child."

I nod.

"Did it help, Kate?"

I shrug a shoulder, trying not to disturb Arleth. "She's a beautiful little girl. She has green eyes like Gage and long brown hair."

"She sounds lovely."

Olivia's phone buzzes. She drops her gaze to it. "It's a reminder of our dinner reservation."

I stare down at Arleth. "Do they deliver? I'm pretty content at the moment."

"I'll order something for us." She smiles. "I don't want to interrupt Aunt Kate and Arleth time."

I pinch my eyes shut to ward off tears. *Aunt Kate*. That's who I'll be to this precious little girl when she's old enough to speak.

Olivia steps away to call the restaurant, so I softly sing a lullaby to Arleth.

I love her with everything I am and I'm just her faux Aunt. I can't imagine what Gage must feel for Kristin.

"Let's change the subject," Olivia begins as she pockets her phone. "Did you take my advice and jump all over Preston the other night?"

I chuckle. "No."

"Why not? The best way to get over one man is to get it on with another."

I shake my head, shielding my smile with a dip of my chin. "I'm not feeling a spark with him, Liv. I met him last night to tell him that."

"So that's over?"

"It's over." Arleth stirs. I rock her softly as I elaborate, "I didn't want to lead him on. He's a great guy."

"There's still a spark somewhere inside of there for Gage, isn't there?" She points at my chest.

I look down at the front of the light blue dress I'm wearing. "There shouldn't be after all this time, should there?"

"I'll take that as a yes."

"It's not a yes."

"It's a no?" She volleys back.

"I don't know," I answer honestly.

I've thought about Gage a lot since last night. If I'm being honest, he's all I've thought about since I left Tin Anchor and went across town to Easton Pub to break off my not-quite-dating relationship with Preston.

"You know." Her head snaps to the right at the sound of a knock on the boutique's doors. "They said they'd have the food here in no time. They weren't kidding."

"My credit card is in my purse." I gesture toward my office with my chin.

"I have cash." She leans down to root around in her bag for her wallet. "Tonight is my treat."

Chapter 23

Gage

The sight in front of me catches my breath in my throat.

Katie is sitting on a bench in the showroom of her bridal store. Her long hair is tied up into a ponytail, revealing the soft contours of her jawline and cheekbones.

She looks peaceful and happy.

I'm guessing the baby swaddled in the pink blanket in her arms has everything to do with it.

She's humming softly as the baby sleeps.

"Kate." The woman who opened the door to the boutique calls out. "Someone is here to see you."

She knows exactly who I am. She called me by name when she opened the door to let me in.

"You're Gage Burke," she drawled.

I heard the surprised disappointment in her voice.

"Who?" Katie's head pops us, her eyes zeroing in on me immediately.

"Him." The woman with the dark hair jerks her thumb at me.

"I hoped that you'd still be here." I take a step closer to Katie. "I wanted to say something."

"I'm busy." She glances at the baby in her arms. "I'm having dinner with my friend."

"Olivia Donato." The woman next to me bumps her shoulder against my bicep. "I'm Kate's friend. I'm one of her best friends."

I sense a subtle threat woven into her words.

I glance at her. "It's good to meet you, Olivia."

She tosses me a look that tells me that I need to watch my step around Katie. It's obvious that Olivia knows about our past.

"I don't want to interrupt," I say even though it's a lie. "There's something I'd like to discuss, Katie. If you let me know when you have time, I can come back."

"She'll call you," Olivia says.

I look down at her. "She doesn't have my number."

Her eyes lock on mine. She studies my face carefully. "Do you have her number?"

"I'm swamped right now," Katie interjects, rocking the baby in her arms. "We have new shipments coming in every day and we're booked solid with appointments. I have to spend every second on work. I don't have time right now to…"

"Give me your phone." Olivia's hand darts out.

I don't ask what the hell is going on. I slide my phone out of the pocket of my jeans and drop it in her palm.

"What are you doing?" Katie struggles to get to her feet without waking the sleeping infant. "Olivia, don't."

Olivia's fingers skim over the screen of my phone. They stop when she reaches the contact list.

She looks up at me, her eyes widening. "Is this Kate's old number? This was her number in California?"

I glance down at my phone and the open tab on my contact list.

Katie.

The picture above her name is one I took the day after I asked her to marry me. We were at the beach. Katie's blonde hair is wind kissed. Her cheeks are pink. The smile on her face exudes pure happiness.

The L.A. based ten-digit phone number below her name was disconnected five years ago.

I nod. "It was."

Something passes over Olivia's face with my confirmation. The veil of anger drops. It's replaced with something softer. I'd call it understanding, but it might be pity.

"I'm going to give him your number." Olivia turns her attention to Kate. "He already knows how to reach you here at the store."

Resignation loosens Katie's shoulders. "Fine."

Olivia deletes the California number, replacing it with a number with a Manhattan area code.

She hands the phone back to me. "Text her something so she has your number too."

"I will."

I have no intention of doing it while Olivia's watching my every move.

I'm glad Katie has such a fierce and loyal friend.

"I'll take off now." I look over at Katie. "I'll be in touch if that's all right with you?"

She looks to Olivia, before her gaze lands on my face. "It's all right with me."

I may have walked in this store hoping to smooth over what happened between us last night at Tin Anchor, but I'm walking out with Katie's phone number.

A few weeks ago I wondered if I'd ever see her again, so I call this a win.

***

Gage: *Do you still like poetry, Katie?*

This has to be the thirtieth fucking message I've typed in the last two hours. I deleted the other twenty-nine before I hit the send button.

I bite the bullet and let fate take the wheel.

I exhale harshly once it's sent.

A response comes quickly.

Kate: *Who is this?*

I don't know if I should be laughing or cursing.

Gage: *It's me. Gage.*

I take a drink from the bottle of water in front of me and gaze around the interior of Tin Anchor. We're at full capacity tonight. I brought Zeke in to handle the overflow. I was too focused on the fact that I have Katie's number. It's a gift that I don't want to fuck up.

Minutes pass before a response lights up my phone.

Kate: *Why did you come to my store tonight?*

I doubt like hell that I can explain that in a text message. It's a face-to-face conversation I want so I push for that.

Gage: *Would you be willing to meet me for a coffee tomorrow?*

This time she types out an immediate reply.

Kate: *I can't. I'm busy tomorrow.*

Gage: *The day after?*

One of my regular customers approaches with a four-person drink order. He's brought his out-of-town in-laws to the bar. I slide my phone into my pocket to prepare the order while I chat with him about the must-see sights in the city.

My phone is back in my palm the second he drops a tip into the jar on the bar in front of me.

I curse under my breath when I see there's nothing from Katie.

My thumbs linger over my phone's screen. I want to type out another message telling her that I can't stop thinking about her. I want to confess everything to her, including her part in my life these past five years, but I stop myself.

She didn't sign up for this.

I turn up the volume on my phone to the highest setting and pocket it again.

She didn't tell me to go straight to hell so I know there's something left in her heart for me too. This isn't over.

It might just be a new beginning.

Chapter 24

Kate

I waited five days before I replied to Gage's text message.

Part of the delay was because of work. A lot was going on at the boutique including an appointment with the mayor's daughter. She's a celebrity in her own right since she landed a prime position as the lead anchor on one of the national morning shows.

We worked out an agreement a few weeks ago that would allow a camera crew access to the boutique to capture the moment she found her dream dress.

It didn't go as planned.

It took three days and over a hundred dresses to find one that she loved.

Once the segment airs next week, I know business will pick up even more.

I admit that I did look at Gage's text messages at least a few times a day.

When I finally did text him back this morning, he was the one who suggested we meet at Palla on Fifth after I was done work. It's a café on Fifth Avenue that makes the best cup of coffee in the city.

I look down at the faded jeans, white blouse and heeled sandals I'm wearing. I stopped at home after work so I could change out of the plum sheath dress I had on. I needed the time to decompress.

Olivia called to check in on me just as I was leaving my apartment. We haven't talked about Gage since the night he showed up at the boutique.

After he left, she told me that she had given him my number because she could tell that things aren't completely settled between us.

Today, she followed that up with a stern warning about watching myself when I'm around him.

"Sort your past, Kate, and keep your wits about you whenever you see him. He's too handsome for his own good."

I didn't bother arguing with her.

I swing open the glass door of the café and spot my ex-fiancé immediately. He's sitting alone at a small circular table, his fingers tugging on the beads of the bracelet on his left wrist.

I take a moment to watch him.

Olivia was right when she said he's too handsome for his own good. I've always thought he was the best-looking man I'd ever seen. The past five years haven't changed my opinion on that.

The first time he kissed me, I felt something inside of me crack open as if a match had been taken to it.

I lit up. Every cell in my body came alive.

My experiences with intimacy up to that point were confined to kissing and some touching. I'd felt a man's hands on my skin, but never to the point of an orgasm.

My first kiss with Gage changed everything. I almost came from the taste of his lips and his hands squeezing my ass.

We made love for the first time a month later. It was tender and everything I needed. Gage was compassionate and loving.

After that, some days we'd go at each other like we were starved. Our fucking would be frantic and quick, driven by our desperate need to feel each other.

Other times, we'd take it slow. Hours would pass while we savored each touch and taste.

I craved all of it.

He stands when he sees me, revealing a pair of dark gray pants, a black belt, and a white button-down shirt. The sleeves are rolled up to his elbows.

He raises his hand in the air in a greeting, drawing glances from the women sitting at nearby tables.

I feel the same magnetic pull toward him that's always been there, so I go to him, sensing that the conversation we're about to have will change everything.

***

I sip from the white ceramic coffee mug as I watch Gage watch me.

"What's the deal with you and Preston?"

His question catches me off-guard. I take a deep breath, trying to mask the surprise in my tone. "Preston?"

"The guy you're seeing." Disdain colors his words. "How serious is that?"

I could resort back to my standard *that's none of your damn business* response, but I opt for honesty. "That's over."

"Over?" He doesn't bother hiding the wicked grin on his mouth. "Who ended that?"

"You didn't just ask me that," I quip.

He doesn't say a thing as a barista approaches us with a carafe of coffee in one hand and a wicker basket filled with cream cups and sugar packets in the other. "Would either of you like a refill?"

I wave a hand over the top of my cup. "I'm good."

She turns her attention to Gage. "Sir?"

"Please," he says to her even though his gaze is pinned to me.

She makes small talk about the weather as she fills his cup. Her eyes linger on his face for a beat too long before she finally walks away, leaving us alone again.

"What's running through your mind right now, Katie?"

That's a loaded question. I blurt out the first thing that I can think of. "When did you move to New York?"

"Six months ago." He taps his fingertips on the table.

I stick with the current line of questioning even though he's the one who invited me here. "Why did you move to New York?"

"Something inside of me told me that this is the place I needed to be."

I smile at that answer. It's something twenty-four-year-old Gage would have said. Back then, he had a vision that included a medical degree, summer weekends spent on his parents' sailboat, and trips to Paris for our wedding anniversaries.

Neither of us had been to France when he proposed the idea, but he said that something inside of him had sparked an urge to visit the City of Lights with his bride.

We were supposed to celebrate our honeymoon there. The trip was a wedding gift from his mom and dad.

"I like it here." A beat passes as he takes a sip of coffee. "It's starting to feel more and more like home to me."

That says a lot. Gage loved Los Angeles. When we met, he was the quintessential California guy with a surfboard under one arm and glowing bronzed skin.

He studied like mad but always made time to be on the water.

The ocean lured him to its shores. That's why he loved taking me sailing on Sunday afternoons.

It was a place where we could be alone without the pressures of parents who had plotted out our lives for us.

"Do you like it here, Katie?"

I don't hesitate before I answer, "I love it here."

We never spoke about New York City when we were together. The plan was to settle down in California and build a life for two. It's ironic that we're sitting across from each other in a coffee shop in the east coast city we both now live in.

"We were both destined to come here." He sits up straighter.

"This isn't fate, Gage. It's a coincidence."

A cocky smile curls his lips. "Call it what you will, but we're in the same place now and I believe there's a reason for that."

Chapter 25

Gage

She doesn't give me an inch. That's the Katie that I've always known. She's the woman I've always loved.

She eyes me up, taking in every word I just said.

Blind belief in the concept of fate isn't a foundation to build your dreams on, but I've held to it to get me through some of the darkest days of my life.

I knew that eventually I'd see her beautiful face again.

"Are you going to tell me that you know what that reason is?" she asks the question with a smirk.

What I'd give to kiss that off her lips.

"There's a lot left unsaid between us." I start there because it's safe and it opens the door for her to give me the hell I deserve.

"What's left to say?" She holds my gaze.

I'm tempted to jump in with both feet and tell her that I'm still in love with her, but those words are better kept to myself at the moment.

"I was an asshole to you."

"Agreed," she snaps back with a slight smile.

"You deserved better," I continue my list of confessions.

"So much better," she chimes in, tapping her manicured fingernail on the rim of the coffee cup in front of her.

"I should have told you about Kristin."

"Why didn't you?"

I won't push the blame for that decision back on her. She made it clear months before I proposed to her that she didn't want to be a mom. That made it easy to walk away with my secret intact the day I ended our engagement.

"Shock," I admit. "I needed time to process it."

"That's why you went out on your parents' boat."

There's no question in her statement. She knew me better than I knew myself when we were together. Whenever life got too heavy, I'd hit the open water.

It's a place where I find peace. I can sort my thoughts as I stare at the waves. I tried to do that after Madison told me I was Kristin's dad. It's the only time in my life I got back to shore with more questions than answers.

"I thought it would help me, but it just fucked me up more." I push my coffee cup to the side and rest my hands on the table. "Once I docked the boat I came looking for you."

The cup in her hand stops in mid-air. She lowers it, keeping her eyes pinned on me. "You came looking for me?"

I didn't have to be a mind reader to know that her family didn't relay any of the messages I left with them. I tried both her parents first, but that took me nowhere fast.

Her mother hung up as soon as I said my name. Her dad took the time to tell me to fuck the hell off. That came with a threat about breaking most of the bones in my body.

Mr. Wesley isn't a violent man. He wouldn't have brought an angry hand to me.

His words were grounded in his daughter's grief.

I got that, so I turned my attention to Eldred, Katie's brother.

"I stopped at our apartment, but you'd moved out," I say, shoving a hand through my hair. "I took everything you left behind."

"That's why you have those things," she mutters.

"I talked to your parents and Eldred."

"You did?" The surprise in her tone confirms that they never mentioned my calls to her.

"Your parents wanted nothing to do with me, " I stop for a beat before I go on, "understandably so. I hurt you."

She nods. "What about Eldred?"

"I finally caught up with him four months after we broke up." I don't correct myself. I'm the ass who broke up with her. Ending our relationship wasn't her decision. That was all on me. "I tracked him down at the gym when I took Kristin to California to visit my parents."

Her index finger traces the rim of the coffee cup in front of her. It's a motion meant to calm her. The repeated movement of her hand is familiar to me. I'd catch her hand in mine when I'd notice her doing it when we lived together.

I'd quiet her unease with assurances whispered in her ear about how brave she was or how smart she was. There wasn't an obstacle that stood a chance against her inner strength once it was ignited.

"What did he say to you?"

"He told me you moved to Denver." I huff out a laugh. "I left Kristin with my parents and I headed straight to the airport."

"You thought I went to work at the office there?"

Her father branched out just months after I left town. It made sense that Katie had moved to Colorado to oversee the new operations.

"I hoped," I admit. "I kept pushing but Eldred told me you were happy and I needed to drop it."

"You believed him?" she quizzes with a hand on her chin. "You believed him when he told you that?"

"No," I answer succinctly.

"No?"

"You love me, Katie. I knew you couldn't be happy without me."

She laughs. "I'm happy without you."

"You're not," I snap back with a smile.

"I am." She pushes back from the table. "You don't know what makes me happy anymore, Gage."

"I make you happy."

She shakes her head. "You haven't in a very long time. What we had is over. It's been over for years. You get that, right?"

"It's not over," I say confidentially. "I'm still crazy about you. You're still just as wild about me."

"This is ridiculous." She shoulders her purse. "We haven't seen each other in five years. There's nothing left between us."

"Prove it."

That takes her to her feet. "Prove it? What the hell is that supposed to mean?"

I'm out of my chair too and in front of her before she realizes what's happening. "Kiss me."

Her gaze drops to my lips. "You're insane."

"Kiss me and prove that there's nothing left between us."

"I am not kissing you," she hisses out between her cherry red lips.

"Kiss me," I demand again as I take a step closer.

Her breath gusts over my chin. "No."

My hands move to her upper arms. I feel the warmth of her skin as her eyelids flutter shut.

When she opens them, her gaze is pinned to my mouth. "I don't want to kiss you."

"You do."

The corners of her lips curve up. "I don't."

I slide one hand up her neck until I'm cradling the back of it. "Kiss me, Katie. If you feel nothing, I swear to God I'll leave you alone."

Her tongue darts over her bottom lip before she bunches the front of my dress shirt into her right fist, yanks me forward and crashes her sweet mouth into mine.

Chapter 26

Kate

How the hell can his kiss still do things to me?

I part my lips when his tongue brushes against them. He groans into my mouth exactly the way he used to.

My knees don't stand a chance.

I stumble toward him with the front of his shirt bunched in one fist, and my other hand snaking its way through his hair.

My common sense is telling me to stop, but every other part of my body is begging me to keep going.

His hand tightens its grip on my neck while the other inches down my back toward my ass.

If he touches it, I'll be lost to this.

Our kiss breaks when I draw up the strength to pull back.

"Katie." My name tumbles from his full lips in a rush. "Jesus, Katie."

I struggle to even my breathing with his forehead pressed against mine.

"That was…shit…that was fucking amazing." He huffs out a deep laugh. "You do things to me."

I feel it.

I know he's hard as stone beneath his pants.

His erection is pressed against me, taunting me, teasing me.

I curse inwardly. I can't think about us in bed together.

I step back, instantly feeling bereft when his hands drop to his sides.

He stares at me, watching my fingers as they strum over my lips.

"You felt that," he accuses with a cocky smile. "You felt what I felt."

I shake my head a little too vigorously. "No. I didn't."

His gaze lands on the front of my blouse. "Your body says otherwise."

I know my nipples have peaked into hard points. I cross my arms over my chest. "We shouldn't have done that."

"We needed to do that," he counters. "You can't tell me that you don't want me still."

I can. I should, but it would be a lie.

The man broke my heart, but he still knows how to awaken something inside of me. The longing for his touch is real.

I glance at the door to the café. "I have to go."

"Home?" he asks, lowering his voice. "Are you going home?"

"I'm going somewhere," I answer because I need to talk to Tilly or Olivia.

Tilly will tell me to jump back into bed with Gage. Olivia will offer a more cautious opinion about guarding my heart.

I don't know what piece of advice I need more right now.

"You'll have dinner with me soon," he says with a tilt of his head. "You still love shrimp scampi, don't you?"

I ignore everything he just said as I fish in my purse for my phone. Once it's in my palm, I hold it to my chest as if it contains all the answers to the questions racing through me.

Gage nods his chin toward my phone. "I'll call you tomorrow."

I don't say anything. I turn, stumble my first step and then head straight for the door as I type out a three-word text message with my shaking hands.

Kate: *I kissed him.*

***

"Tell me everything." Tilly smiles as she tucks my hair behind my shoulder. "You look flushed. Is that from kissing Gage or did you run all the way here from Palla's?"

I glance around the vet clinic. The waiting room is packed with dogs, cats, two birds, and at least a dozen people.

I run a hand over my forehead. "You're busy. I can wait. We can talk about this when you're done work."

Her gaze drops to the watch on my wrist. "I punched out thirty minutes ago. Sebastian has a meeting, so I'm hanging out here until he's done."

I suddenly realize that I just assumed that Tilly would drop everything to counsel me about what I should do next. I should have asked if she had plans tonight when she responded to the text I sent her announcing that I'd kissed Gage.

She told me to get my ass down to Premier Pet Care, so that's what I did.

"It's always a zoo on the nights we're open late." She points at the waiting room. "I thought I might be able to help Dr. Hunt, but two other vet techs are here, so I'm free to go. Let's grab a drink."

I need a drink. I need anything that will take the edge off.

"You have time?" I reach for her hand. "I don't want to take you away from your husband."

"He'll be at least another hour." She shrugs. "We're going to grab some Italian take-out, hold hands on the subway and then eat spaghetti before we practice baby-making."

I laugh. "Are you still in practice mode with the baby-making?"

"I'm still on birth control." She pats her flat stomach. "Next year we'll put all our practice to good use."

Tilly's desire to have a child is buried beneath the joy she's experiencing being a newlywed.

Sebastian is on the same page. A baby will happen when they're both ready.

"One martini." I hold up my index finger. "My treat."

"I'll grab my purse." She rounds the reception desk to head back to the staff room. "I'm dying to know about this kiss, Kate. I think you just took the first step toward your second chance with Gage."

I reached out to Tilly for a reason.

She won't tell me to put Gage in my rearview mirror and move on with my life. There won't be any warnings about the high probability that he'll break my heart again.

She'll talk about true love, throwing caution to the wind, and exploring all the possibilities.

I need that tonight because that kiss sparked something deep within me that I thought had died five years ago.

Reaching up to touch my kiss-swollen lips, I feel hope fluttering in my chest.

Chapter 27

Gage

"You kissed your old flame?" Dylan Colt, my attorney and friend, lifts the bottle in his hand in the air. "That sounds like a reason to celebrate."

I tap the side of his beer bottle with my water bottle. "Give me more of a reason, Dylan. Tell me you've got good news for me."

I didn't plan on meeting up with him tonight. I would have been just fine on my own, reliving that kiss I shared with Katie earlier.

I had to rest my ass back in the chair after she left Palla on Fifth. My dick was hard as stone and my vision was blurring from the constant thundering of my heart inside my chest.

I almost took off after her, but I knew she needed space.

The kiss impacted her just as much as it did me.

When Dylan called to tell me that he was here at Tin Anchor looking for me, I got on the subway.

"I'm doing everything in my power to bring you good news." He sets the bottle on the bar.

"Good," I reply, wishing he had something more to offer today. "I need to see my daughter."

"I'm working on that." His gaze drops to his phone. "I told you when you first came to see me that I would put everything I had into reuniting you with Kristin. Nothing's changed."

I hired Dylan to help me navigate the muddy waters of Kristin's custody because he's the best divorce attorney in Manhattan.

Even though Madison and I never married, it doesn't make our situation any less complicated.

In fact, it's fucking complex. Every minute that passes is another moment in time that I don't get to share with my daughter.

Dylan tugs on the lapels of his gray suit jacket. The guy invests a small fortune in his wardrobe. His black hair is cut with precision. He's what you'd expect a textbook version of an attorney to look like.

His tactics are cutthroat though which is why I sought him out after a regular at the bar sung his praises. She told me that Dylan had accomplished something that the three attorneys she'd hired before him couldn't. Dylan got her shared custody of her kids after two judges had ruled she'd have no visitation.

He's a miracle worker. I'm counting on him using those skills to get me face-to-face with Kristin.

"Tell me about the old flame." He takes a pull of beer. "I take it that it's Katie you kissed?"

Her name came up one night when Dylan and I took to the pool table. A few good shots with the pool cue and even more of tequila got me loosened up enough that story-after-story about Katie poured out of me.

Dylan listened and then mentioned a girl he met in high school. He didn't expand on that. I didn't push.

I've only known him a few months, but I've watched him strike up conversations with women when he's been here at the bar. He has a type; light brown hair, blue eyes, pretty and petite. He's left with every woman he's bought a drink for.

Tonight, he's more focused on the imported bottle of beer in his hand than any of the women looking in his direction.

"We met for coffee. Things progressed from there." I keep the details to a minimum.

I haven't told Dylan that Katie lives in Manhattan. He put those pieces together himself when he overheard me mentioning her to Myles one night last week.

Myles parked himself on a stool next to Dylan and promptly asked if I'd gotten Katie back into bed yet. I told him to go to hell, he laughed and ordered a scotch. Dylan got up to take a call.

As if on cue, his phone rings.

"Fuck." He hangs his head. "It's too late for this shit."

I huff out a laugh. "When I handed over my retainer to you, you told me you were available day and night. Some people take that literally."

"Thanks for not being one of them." His gaze drops to the phone's screen. "It's a client. She's under the impression she can pay me in blow jobs."

I shake my head. I've heard it before. He's got more than a few stories to tell of recently divorced women throwing their naked selves at his feet in his office.

"You're not answering that?" I tilt my chin toward his phone.

"I don't fuck clients." His gaze wanders to the end of the bar where a woman with light brown hair is sipping from a glass filled with vodka and cranberry juice.

"You have no problem fucking my customers," I point out as his phone quiets.

He tosses the woman a smile. "Not tonight. I'm due in court bright and early. I'm heading back to my office to prep."

"You'll keep me updated on my case?" I ask as I clear his empty bottle from the bar top.

"The second I have news, I'll call." Standing, he opens his wallet and drops a twenty dollar bill on the bar. "I'm not giving up, Gage. You sure as hell better not."

"I'll fight until my dying breath for my little girl." I exhale harshly. "I'll never give up on her."

He stalks toward the door, ignoring the woman at the end of the bar with her eyes pinned on him.

She's off her stool and trailing him before his foot hits the sidewalk.

My hand dives into the front pocket of my jeans. I tug out my phone and glance at the screen. The only missed message is from Myles.

I didn't expect to hear from Katie. It might be days before she reaches out, but that kiss held promise and she felt it too. There's no way in hell she can ignore that.

Chapter 28

Kate

Guilt crawls up my skin as I stand outside Tin Anchor.

It's not because I rushed out of Palla on Fifth last night to see Tilly.

I needed her romantic view of what could be between Gage and me. We spent more than an hour talking about how the kiss made me feel.

It was a flashback to college when I raced over to Mariah Larson's dorm room to tell her that I'd kissed Gage Burke.

I'll never forget the flicker of disappointment on my friend's face before she screamed in delight.

Six months later I found out that Mariah wanted him.

Tilly doesn't want Gage. Last night, it was all about how I felt.

When I was with Tilly at a bar down the street from Premier Pet Care, I confessed that the kiss had curled my toes and sparked something that I haven't felt in five years.

When I went home, my hand dove into my panties and I got off to the memory of Gage inside of me.

In my imagination, his thrusts were strong and wild. He breathed heavy on my neck, whispering that he loved how good I felt.

This morning, I swore to myself that I'd forget the kiss ever happened.

By noon, I was dreaming about another one.

It's eight p.m. now and I'm wondering why the hell I'm standing on this sidewalk and not at home, thinking about anything but my ex-fiancé and how incredible it feels to kiss him.

I shouldn't have touched myself last night. I definitely shouldn't have done it with images of Gage's naked body dancing in my mind.

"Katie?"

The deep timbre of Gage's voice shoots right to my core. I close my eyes to ward off the memory of him growling out my name when I had his cock in my mouth for the first time years ago.

I thought he was inside the bar, but he's standing behind me.

I swipe a hand over my forehead and turn to face him.

Dammit.

The man can make anything look good, especially a pair of jeans, a black T-shirt and a panty-dropping smile.

I inch my hand over my hip to make sure my lace panties are still in place under my pink dress.

"Gage," I say his name to give myself a second to find some composure.

"It's good to see you." His gaze drops to the front of my wrap dress.

I know my nipples have hardened, even though the temperature is hovering around eighty degrees.

I don't repeat the sentiment to him because I know he'll comment about how he can tell that I'm happy to see him.

I need to invest in something other than thin lace bras.

"Can I make you a drink?" He gestures to the door of Tin Anchor. "A dirty martini with two olives."

I tug on the silver hoop earring in my left ear. "I came to say that the kiss was a mistake."

His lips twist back into a smile. "No, you didn't."

Gage always wore arrogance like a badge. Obviously, that hasn't changed.

"I did." I drop my hands to my hips. "We shouldn't have kissed."

He takes a measured step closer to me. "We should kiss again."

We should.

I bite my bottom lip to stop myself from saying that.

"I'll make you a drink and we'll talk." He gestures to the handle on the door. "You didn't come here because you felt nothing last night."

"One drink," I reply because I won't give any more weight to his words about what I did or didn't feel.

He moves past me to yank open the door to his bar. "One drink and we'll go from there."

***

Two martinis later and my self-control has disappeared.

I don't try to hide the fact that I'm staring at Gage's muscular arms as he prepares a tray of drinks for a female server who can't take her eyes off of him.

Jealousy charges through me like a herd of wild horses.

I have no claim on the man.

He hasn't been mine in five years.

He can flirt with anyone, kiss anyone, fuck anyone.

I scowl at the thought of him taking the server to his apartment and devouring her in his bed.

He looks in my direction, his gaze catching mine.

We haven't had a chance to talk yet. He took over for Zeke when we first arrived and since there's a baseball game on TV tonight, the bar is packed.

I've been nursing my drinks and texting my mom. She still has no idea that Gage has popped back into my life.

I was tempted to confront her and my dad about why they didn't tell me that Gage reached out after our broken engagement, but it's water under the bridge at this point.

They did what they thought was best for me at the time. They were trying to help me navigate my grief in the best way they knew how.

Gage approaches me with a white bar towel in his hands. "You have that look on your face."

I run my fingers over my top lip. "What look?"

"You're jealous."

What the hell?

"I haven't slept with her. I won't be sleeping with her."

"With who?" I ask in my best, slightly tipsy but nonchalant voice.

It comes out at a much higher pitch than I intended.

"Callie. She's Zeke's sister. She comes in a few times a week to help out." He rests both of his forearms on the bar and leans closer to me.

I tap a finger to my forehead. "I'll make a note of that right here."

A smile floats over his mouth. "Are you drunk?"

A giggle bubbles out of me, which prompts a laugh from him.

His gaze narrows. "Did you eat anything tonight?"

I wiggle two fingers in the air. "I had two chocolate chip cookies before I came here. I keep the package in my desk drawer."

My hand jumps to cover my mouth. What the actual fuck is wrong with me? Why would I confess that?

His full lips curve up into a sly grin. "You used to hide the package in the bottom drawer of your nightstand."

"You knew about that?"

"The crumbs in the bed and the chocolate at the corner of your mouth were dead giveaways." He reaches up to swipe the pad of his thumb over my bottom lip. "I loved that you thought you could keep a secret from me. You never could, Katie."

I could. I did.

"Do you still like your pizza with extra pepperoni?" He glances at the door of the bar as a group of people crowd in. "The place across the street makes a good slice. I'll run and get you a couple."

I shake my head. "I have leftover pizza at home. I'll go have that."

A sudden wave of dizziness hits me as I slide off the barstool. I reach forward to steady myself, but it's his hand I catch, not the edge of the bar.

"Sit," he says, squeezing my hand. "I'll get Callie to tend bar. I'm taking you home."

I drop his hand and lower myself back onto the stool.

There's no harm in him taking me home if I don't invite him up to my apartment.

I tell myself that as he flashes me a killer smile. I look away, vowing that I'll never kiss him again even though I know it's a lie.

Chapter 29

Gage

I wouldn't have pegged Katie for an Upper West Side resident.

Back in California we lived in a neighborhood teeming with activity. The street she lives on now is quiet with large trees and buildings with doormen.

As soon as we left Tin Anchor, she started in about how she was fine on her own. She had too much to drink and too little to eat tonight.

I couldn't leave her be, not just because it would have been an asshole move, but I wanted to see where she lived.

I've been imagining her in a walk-up in Tribeca, not here.

"I'm just down the block." She waves her right hand in the air in front of her. "I can make it from here on my own."

I have every confidence in that. I'm also damn sure that she wants to kiss me again.

Her eyes were glued to my mouth on the subway. I was on the phone with Myles talking about his upcoming bachelor party.

I ignored my ringing phone twice before Katie insisted that I answer it.

When we stepped off the train, I was next to her.

The ache to reach out and grab her hand was real, but I shoved both of mine into the front pockets of my jeans to avoid the temptation.

Years back, our hands would instinctively find each other whenever we were side-by-side.

"I'll walk you to the door," I offer with a smile.

She mumbles something under her breath as she glances up at me.

I've been doing most of the talking since we stepped off the subway.

I started with a comment about the busker playing a guitar and crooning a Frank Sinatra tune.

She headed straight for him when she heard him singing. His version of the classic earned him a five-dollar tip from her and a smile.

The fact that he thanked her with a misplaced bow and a cheery accented, "Thank you, Lady Kate," told me that she stopped to listen to him before today.

Once we hit the sidewalk to walk the two blocks to her place, I brought up the weather and the never-ending construction in the city.

She didn't add anything to the conversation other than an occasional shrug of her shoulder and a raise of her brow.

She's nervous-as-hell. It's written all over her face.

She comes to such an abrupt stop that I take a few steps past her before I realize what's happening.

Her thumb jerks to the right and the front of a white-bricked building. "This is it."

I look at the exterior. It's a pre-war building with arched windows, glass panel double doors and a doorman watching our every move.

"Thank you for the drinks," she says in an even tone. "I'd thank you for bringing me home, but I could have made it on my own."

Defiant Katie is hot-as-hell.

Her mascara smudged when she rubbed her fists over her eyes. Her lipstick is long gone and the front of her wrap dress is open a touch more than it was when she first sat down at Tin Anchor.

Every single time she moves just the right way, I catch a glimpse of her pink lace bra.

"You don't want to come up." She shakes her head. "No, wait."

"I want to come up," I blurt out before she can get another word in.

"I meant to say that I don't want you to come up."

I smile as I take a step closer to her. "You want me to come up."

"I'm going to eat pizza," she announces with a tilt of her head. "We're not going to do anything."

I motion to the glass doors. "I'll watch you eat pizza."

"I know this is a bad idea," she whispers as she taps the middle of her forehead. "Think about this, Katie."

I haven't heard her self-talk in over five years. It's the only time she refers to herself as Katie. From what I remember, I'm the only person who called her that.

That might have changed. I'm hoping it hasn't.

"I'll make you some coffee." I point at a finger at her. "You'll eat pizza. I'll go home."

"Coffee, pizza, home," she repeats back, studying my face.

I nod.

Her gaze darts from me to the doors. "I saw your apartment, so I guess it's only fair that you see mine."

I fucked this up years ago so I don't think fair fits into this equation, but I'll take it.

"Follow me," she announces as she steps toward the door. "It's coffee, pizza and then home. You promised."

I know what I said. I'll take my leave after coffee and pizza, but I plan on stealing another kiss before the night is over.

Chapter 30

Gage

I step into her apartment, and I'm instantly blown away by how it reflects Katie's taste.

The walls are painted white. It's a blank canvas for everything else in the space.

A large white sectional sits in the middle of the living room. It's crowded with pink and light blue pillows. A dark blue blanket is folded neatly over one arm.

The coffee table is square and painted gray.

A small dining table sits in the corner, covered by a bright blue tablecloth.

I scan the walls to find pictures of Katie's family. I spot her parents in one. They're standing in Times Square, smiling at the camera. I have no doubt that Katie was behind the lens.

Eldred is in another picture with his wife. At one time, I considered Katie's brother my friend but that bond was broken when I left his sister.

I spot a square silver frame containing a photograph of a baby.

"That's Arleth." Katie drops her keys and purse on the coffee table. "She's my friend's baby."

"Olivia's baby," I say quietly.

"Olivia and Alexander's baby," she corrects me. "Before you ask, that's my friend Tilly and her husband. He's a policeman."

I gaze at the frame next to the photo of Arleth. It's an image of a tall dark-haired man and a pretty brunette woman. The background is this room and the window that overlooks the tree-lined street below.

Katie has built a life here. She's put down roots and started a business.

"I can make coffee," she says, starting toward a small kitchen. "No cream or sugar for you, right?"

A wave of nostalgia hits me.

"You remember?"

The emotion in my voice turns her back around to look at me. "I remember, but you had it like that at Palla on Fifth."

I move to take a seat on the sofa. I had no idea how fucking surreal it would be to see her apartment.

I stare down at the red tulips in a vase on the table.

Katie loved fresh flowers when we were together. I'd buy them once a month and she'd care for them as if they were the most important things in the world. She'd keep them until the petals were dropping and the water was murky.

The sound of movement in the kitchen stops. Quick taps of her heels against the hardwood floor follows.

"Here's some pizza." She shoves a plate at me. "It's too much for just me."

I look down at the two slices of pepperoni pizza. It's a small offering, but I take it with a shaky hand. "Thank you, Katie."

She settles onto the sofa next to me, balancing a plate with one slice on her thighs. "The coffee is brewing. One cup and you'll go home, right?"

I want to stay. I want to fucking stay and put my head in her lap while she reads poetry to me and then I want to make love to her.

"One cup and I'll take off," I answer with a smile.

"Eat." She points at the plate in my hand. "I heated yours in the microwave. I know how much you hate cold pizza."

I hate that this moment has to end.

I take a bite of the lukewarm pizza. I chew, not giving a shit that it tastes horrible.

I'm inside the apartment of the woman I love, sharing a meal with her.

This is more than I could have dreamed of.
This is everything.

It's the best night of my life in more than five years.

***

"I had too much to drink." Katie presses her index fingers into her temples. "I'm going to have a massive headache tomorrow morning."

She's sobering up, slowly.

She had one cup of coffee and half of another. I got her the refill adding a splash of cream to it.

The cool rush of evening air flooding the room through the open window is helping clear her head.

I know I should say goodnight, but I'm not ready to leave.

There are a million things I want to say to her, but now is not the time.

"Why don't you live in London?"

"London?" The surprise in my tone is evident. The question feels like it blindly came at me from left field.

"Your daughter lives in London." She crosses her legs. "Why don't you live there?"

I'm not welcome there. I was arrested during my only trip to London. I attempted to see my daughter. The police were called. Dylan's associate there secured my release with the caveat that I would board a plane back to the United States.

"It's a complicated situation," I say with a shake of my head. "I've hired an attorney here. He's working with a lawyer there. I'm hoping they can get me more time with Kristin."

It's not a direct answer, but it's enough to appease her for now.

Her head bobs up and down. "You miss her, don't you?"

"Every moment of every day."

"I hope you get to see her soon," she offers on a sigh.

"Me too."

Sipping from the coffee cup, she watches me intently.

Once the mug is back on the table, her fingers drift to her bottom lip. "I did come to Tin Anchor tonight to talk about that kiss."

"Do you regret kissing me?" I ask even though I know she's likely going to lie and say she does.

I wouldn't be sitting on her sofa, drinking coffee if that were true.

She takes a deep breath. "What do you think?"

She's opening a door that I've been waiting for. I lean closer, inching my hand across my thigh until it brushes against her leg. "I think you liked the kiss more than you want to admit."

Her gaze drops to my hand. "Why would you think that?"

I thicken under the fabric of my jeans. Being this close to her is bordering on unbearable. The kiss only stoked the longing that's been inside of me since I walked out of her life five years ago.

I squeeze her thigh. "You kissed me like you wanted me."

She turns to look at me, her hazel eyes filled with the same need I feel. "I used to want you."

My hand inches higher. "You want me now."

"I don't think I do," she says under her breath. "I think the martinis are clouding my judgment. I'm confused."

I run a fingertip against the soft skin of her inner thigh. "You're not confused."

She leans closer, her sweet breath skirting over my cheek. "You think you still know me."

"I know your body," I bite out between clenched teeth.

I'm so fucking hard. I want more. Jesus, I want to open her dress, pull down her panties and taste her sweet pussy.

I have craved that taste every day for the last five years.

"I'm not the same woman I was back then." Her gaze drops to my hand again, but she makes no move to stop me. "You don't know my body the way you used to."

My fingers slide up until I can feel the lace of her panties brush against them. "Is that a challenge?"

The softest moan escapes her, just as her eyelids flutter shut.

I move in, gliding my lips along her jawline. "I'm going to kiss you again, Katie."

With a nod, her lips part, her legs fall open, and my mouth is on hers.

Chapter 31

Kate

I get lost in the kiss.

I'm buried so deeply beneath my desire for Gage that I ignore the incessant knocking I hear.

His fingers crawl higher, lingering against the front of my panties.

I want him to touch me.

I desperately want him to feel how wet I am.

He groans when the knocking starts up again, but this time it's even louder than before.

It's coming from my apartment door.

Someone is on the other side.

I curse inwardly when I pull back from him.

"Are you expecting someone?" he whispers against the flesh of my neck. "If we ignore them maybe they'll go away."

A series of three loud raps on the door draws me to my feet.

I straighten the front of my dress. It's twisted from my squirming and his hands on the skirt.

Maybe the knocking is a sign that I'm not supposed to be kissing him, let alone touching him.

He was just inches away from diving his fingers into my panties.

"I'm coming," I call out to whoever is behind the door.

"How I wish that were true," Gage murmurs as he slides to his feet.

I cover my mouth with my hand to hide my smile.

The knocking starts again, but this time a voice follows it. "Kate? Wally let me up. He said you're home."

Tilly.

"Wally is the doorman," I offer that explanation to Gage even though he didn't ask. "It's my friend. Tilly is here."

Gage's gaze drifts to the picture of Tilly and Sebastian hanging on the wall.

"I need to let her in." My hands run over my hair, smoothing it.

He nods in response, adjusting the front of his jeans. I saw how hard he was right before he kissed me.

If Tilly wasn't paying me a surprise visit right now, I might be laid bare on the couch enjoying Gage's talented tongue.

A shiver runs through me at the thought of coming against his mouth.

I could never get enough of that when we were together. I could never get enough of him.

"Kate?" Tilly calls again. "It's important. Please."

I move quickly, closing the distance between the sofa and the door in just a few steps.

I glance back to Gage before I swing open the door.

Tilly's gaze darts from me to Gage. "Oh, shit."

"Are you all right?" I grab her hand and tug her into my apartment. "What's wrong?"

She raises her hand in a weak wave to Gage. "I'm Kate's best friend. My friends call me Tilly, but my husband calls me Matilda. You can call me either, but Kate always calls me Tilly, so maybe you want to…"

"Tilly," I stop her rambling with a squeeze of her hand. "What are you doing here?"

"I have a pint of gelato." She taps her hand over the front of her large red purse. "Sebastian has a meeting so I thought we could eat gelato and watch a show, but you're busy."

I stare at her.

She studies my face carefully, her eyes narrowing. "I interrupted something, didn't I?"

"No." I wave the notion away with a brush of my hand in the air. "Gage brought me home. We had some pizza."

"You kissed him." She mouths in silence.

I nod. "He was just leaving."

"Oh my God," she whispers. "You kissed him again."

I hear Gage's footsteps as he approaches us from behind. His hand darts past me, brushing my shoulder. "It's good to meet you, Tilly."

"It's my pleasure, Gage." She scoops his hand in hers.

"I'll leave you two alone."

Tilly jerks his hand closer to her. "You're not going anywhere. I brought enough gelato for all of us. I'll get the bowls and the spoons. You two have a seat. Right over there on the sofa; right next to each other."

***

"Do you have condoms?" Tilly whispers to me as we load the bowls and spoons in the dishwasher.

"I have something better." I toss my hair over my shoulder. "I have an annoying best friend. A well-meaning best friend, but she's super annoying right now."

A broad smile takes over her mouth. "I kept him here, didn't I?"

"He should be at home," I point out as I glance over to where Gage is still sitting on the sofa.

He's spent the last hour listening to Tilly talk about all of the furry patients she took care of today.

His gaze kept catching on mine. Part of me was glad he stayed, but the other part wanted him gone so I could talk freely and openly with Tilly about what almost happened earlier.

I would have had sex with Gage if she hadn't shown up.

I know it.

I have zero doubt about that.

"Think of it this way, Kate." Tilly wraps an arm around my shoulder. "You got the kiss out of the way and it was a relief. Just imagine how much better you'll feel once you fuck him."

I shush her with a finger over her lips. "You did not just say that."

She pushes my finger away. "The sexual tension in here almost melted the gelato. It's hot, hot, hot."

"It's not," I argue.

"Take him to bed with you." She gestures down the hallway. "What harm can come from it?"

I'll fall back in love with him.

I'm already halfway there; maybe more than halfway.

"You don't want to get hurt." She tucks a strand of my hair behind my ear. "I know that's holding you back, but you're not the same girl he dumped. You're a kick-ass woman who can handle her emotions."

"Am I?" I question with a laugh.

"You're attracted to him, aren't you?"

I look over to where Gage is sitting. He's thumbing through a bridal magazine that I brought home from work for research.

He's gorgeous. The martinis are out of my system, and I still want him just as badly as I did when he walked into my apartment tonight.

"He's good-looking."

"So sleep with him." She rolls her eyes. "I need to stop hanging out with Olivia. I'm starting to sound like her."

I throw my head back in laughter. "Olivia told me to be careful with my heart."

"I'm with her on that, but this is sex." She turns us both so we're facing Gage. "Maybe you'll get into bed with him and it will be nothing like you remember. He could be a dud."

There's no way in hell that's true. He's the best lover I've ever had and even though I'm afraid to admit it, I crave his touch as desperately now as I did the first time we made love.

"Or maybe once you have sex you'll realize he's the man you're destined to be with," she says quietly. "You won't know until you take the plunge so do it, Kate."

Chapter 32

Gage

If Tilly hadn't shown up tonight, I would have taken Katie right there on her sofa.

I was so close to sliding down her body to taste her.

I sat through gelato and a discussion about Tilly's work. Then I pretended not to notice how long they hung back in the kitchen.

I could hear their muffled voices, but I couldn't make out one damn word.

Tilly took off just now after hugging Katie. She promised that she'd stop by Tin Anchor one night with her husband.

I told her that the first round would be on the house.

That brought a smile to her face.

I like her.

I can tell that she's a good friend to the woman I love.

Katie turns back from the door to face me.

I don't want her to feel uncomfortable about where we were headed earlier, so I step in and offer something I sense she needs. "I'm going to head out too."

"You're leaving?" The surprise in her tone catches me off guard.

I'd question if she wants me to stay, but I don't want there to be an ounce of regret the morning after.

The only thing I want her to feel after we fuck is a need for more.

"I'm going home."

Her hands fist in front of her. "Should we talk about what happened?"

I close the distance between us with measured steps. "The kiss."

"We almost…" her voice trails. "I think we might have done more than kiss if Tilly hadn't stopped by."

"We would have done more than kiss." I bring a hand to her chin. "We would have fucked."

Her lips part, a small moan seeping out between them. "Gage."

I trace her bottom lip with the pad of my thumb. "I want you, Katie."

"It's been a long time since we were together." She looks up into my face. "It wouldn't be the same."

"It would be better." I slide my hand to cup her cheek. "It would be so fucking good."

Her lips thin into a straight line. "You think it would be better because we have more experience now?"

Regret slices through me like a hot knife. I'm the reason she has more experience. It's my fucking fault that she's been with other men.

"Katie." I pause, trying to find the words to tell her that I don't want to look into the past. I want to focus on what's in front of me right now and I want her to do the same thing.

Her eyes lock on mine. "There were a lot, weren't there? It's been five years. You've slept with a lot of women since we…"

"Katie." Her name escapes me in a growl. "Stop."

"I've been with a few men." Her gaze drops. "Just a handful. All of them here in New York."

Christ. Please, fucking stop.

"We don't have to do this." I quiet her with a soft kiss to her lips. "We don't."

"How many, Gage?" Her lips tremble against mine. "Just tell me how many."

I kiss her again, deeper this time. I taste her breath, slide my tongue along hers and claim her with my mouth the way I've wanted to for the past five years.

"Please," she whispers as the kiss breaks. "I have to know."

I gather her close to me, tucking her head under my chin the way I did when I needed her to know the profound depth of my love for her.

My arms circle her. Her hands rest against my back.

"Why won't you tell me?" She sighs.

I lean back so I can look down into her hazel eyes. "Because you'll understand just how fucked up I've been."

Compassion swims in her gaze. "I want to understand. How many?"

I swallow back my hesitation and answer the question. "None, Katie. The last time was with you."

***

Her eyes search mine for something. She's looking for a sign that I'm speaking the truth.

The fact that my cock is hard as stone should be her first clue that I haven't fucked a woman in half a decade.

I tried.

Jesus, did I try.

I never got past a kiss or a handful of a clothed tit.

Not one of the women I've met since I left California could compare to my Katie.

It wasn't a conscious choice to abstain from sex, but that's the journey I took.

I jerked off almost daily to the mental images I stored of Katie's naked body, or her mouth on my cock.

I fucked my hand thinking about being inside her tight pussy.

It was enough because it had to be.

I don't know how long I could have maintained it, but I never thought far ahead. I got through each day with the hope that I'd find her again.

"You haven't been with a woman?" Tears well in the corner of her eyes. "Gage... I don't know what... are you serious?"

I brush a tear from her cheek. "I'm dead serious."

She shakes her head, her gaze dropping to the front of my jeans and the outline of my erection. "I didn't know."

"I tried to find you." I shove a hand through my hair. "I never gave up hope that I would. I was harassing Eldred every few weeks. Eventually, he would have given up your location."

Her mouth drops open.

I know that it's news to her. I haven't brought it up before now because damaging their sibling bond isn't my intention.

I didn't see the need to confess that I still call Eldred. He rarely answers. That doesn't deter me.

"You talk to Eldred?"

"I try." I huff out a laugh. "He's usually too busy to take or return my calls."

"I need to call him." Her gaze darts back to the coffee table where her phone is. "He had no right."

"He loves you," I say because I know that her brother was only trying to protect her. "He thought it was his place to keep you safe."

"From you?" She taps her hand on my chest. "I'm the only one who gets to decide whether I talk to you or not."

"You're talking to me now." I cup her hands in mine and bring them to my mouth. I plant a soft kiss on her palm. "We'll talk until we've said everything that needs to be said."

She looks directly into my eyes. "We will."

I tug her back into my chest, wrapping my arms around her. "I'm going to go so you can sleep."

She nods.

I plant a kiss on the top of her head. "I'll call you soon."

"Tomorrow, Gage?" She tilts her head back to look up at me. "Call me tomorrow."

I press my lips against hers in a slow kiss. "Tomorrow it is."

Chapter 33

Kate

"Marry him," Tilly says, clapping her hands in glee. "He waited for you. Oh my God, he waited for you. This is so romantic."

"Once he gets his hands on you, you won't be able to walk for a week. Five years of pent up sexual need is inside of that man," Olivia jumps in, tossing me a wink.

"That's hot." Tilly fans her hand in front of her face. "The sex is going to be incredible."

I glance down at Arleth sleeping in her stroller. "We shouldn't be talking about this in front of the baby."

"The baby is dreaming about her favorite stuffed bear." Olivia pats a hand over Tilly's forearm. "She loves that bear, Tilly. Thank you again for that."

I sip on the lemonade I ordered after we were seated at an outdoor table.

Olivia called me just after seven this morning with a million questions about Gage. Tilly had texted her on the way home from my apartment last night.

I told her I'd meet her for lunch. She's the one who invited Tilly to join us at one of her favorite restaurants. It's just down the street from Alexander's music school.

"When are you going to take him to bed?" Olivia doesn't pull any punches. "That needs to happen today."

"The sooner the better," Tilly agrees with a nod of her head. "Invite him over to your place tonight. I promise I'll stay home."

I laugh out loud. "It's not happening tonight."

"Why not?" They ask in unison.

I shake my head. "I need time to process everything."

The server approaches with our order of nachos. He strikes up a conversation with Olivia about Alexander's recent interview on a podcast he listens to. It's obvious he knows that Olivia's husband is one of the preeminent orchestra conductors in the world.

Olivia promises that she'll bring her husband in for one lunch day soon. That's enough to get the server to offer a free dessert to each of us.

"I love your husband," Tilly says once the server has walked away. "He's such a big deal that I get a free brownie."

Olivia giggles. "I'm having cheesecake."

I'm having a crisis.

It started last night when Gage confessed that he hasn't had sex in five years.

I tossed and turned the night away thinking about that.

I was hesitant the first time I got into bed with a man after our breakup, but I knew I had to move on.

I enjoyed the sex I've had since our engagement ended. I don't feel guilty about it, although I know I wouldn't have pursued anything with another man if I had known Gage was looking for me.

Eldred got a piece of my mind after Gage left last night and another dose of my anger this morning.

My brother told me that he was looking out for me. He saw the pain I was in after Gage left me, and he wanted to shield me from that.

I get it.

I hate it, but I understand it.

Our bond is strong, but it's going to take time for me to accept what he did.

Maybe Gage and I wouldn't have gotten back together, but we didn't have the chance to explore that because Eldred stood watch over my heart.

"I know that I've been telling you to be careful, Kate." Olivia elbows me. "But I don't know many men who would step away from sex because of a woman they haven't seen in years."

I spread my white linen napkin over my lap, covering my red skirt.

"I think you should throw caution to the wind." Tilly circles her hand in the air. "You only live once. Second chances are rare so take this one and run with it."

A soft whimper from the stroller lures all of our gazes to Arleth's face.

She opens her blue eyes, immediately locking them on her mom.

"We'll continue this discussion later," Olivia says, scooping her daughter into her arms. "I need to feed this little sweetheart and we have to eat the nachos before they get cold. They are Alexander's absolute favorite things in the world. Take a bite and you'll see why."

I dive into lunch and listening mode as Olivia tells us about how close Arleth came to rolling over this morning.

I eat and watch my two best friends interact. They've forged a bond of their own since they met through me. I'm grateful for moments like this when we're altogether.

I'm just about to tell them that when my phone chimes in my purse.

I slide it out and read the simple text message.

Gage: *A penny for your thoughts?*

I stare down at the screen, tears misting my vision.

I look up, but Tilly and Olivia are so focused on the cute noises Arleth is making that they don't notice the emotion that is crashing around me.

I type back the response I always gave him when he asked me that question.

Kate: *A dollar for your dreams?*

I rest my phone in my lap and hold my breath, waiting for him to reply.

Chapter 34

Gage

A dollar for your dreams?

She remembers.

When we lived together in California, I'd write messages to Katie on our bathroom mirror using the tube of red lipstick she always kept in the medicine cabinet.

Sometimes I'd scribble out a simple *I love you* or *Let's fuck*.

The messages were reflective of my mood.

One of them was in the form of a question: *A penny for your thoughts*?

I'd leave that for her when she was quiet or pensive.

She never gave me a direct answer.

It was always a question to counter mine.

She did the same thing today via text.

The urge to call her and tell her that every single one of my dreams involves her is strong, but I drop my phone on the top of the bar and take a breath.

I'm at Tin Anchor early today to take care of some paperwork. The only patron we have is a brown-haired guy in a suit who looks like his world just exploded.

He's on his second glass of whiskey.

He's tight-lipped and moody, but I'm not complaining about the silence.

"I need another," he calls out in a low voice. "Bring me the bottle."

I know better than that. This guy doesn't need another drink. He needs an ear to listen to him gripe about whatever is fucking up his life right now.

I pour him another two fingers of whiskey before I put the bottle back behind the bar.

He downs half the drink in a swallow.

I head back to my phone and type out a response to Katie.

Gage: *My dream at the moment is to cook you dinner tonight. Keep the dollar.*

I press send, trusting that the last three words will bring a smile to her lips.

They did when she was twenty-two and desperately in love with me.

"You're happy." The guy in the suit comments from his bar stool. "It's got to be a woman who put that smile on your face."

The third drink is the charm with this guy. He's finally cracked open.

I walk back to where he's sitting. "It's a woman."

"A woman put me here." He pats the top of the bar. "I never thought I'd get this torn up about her."

I've had this conversation enough times to know that he wants me to ask a follow-up question, so I do. "What's her name?"

"Gina." He exhales. "Gina Calvetti."

I pick up a bar towel and start wiping down a row of wine glasses. "What's Gina Calvetti like?"

"Like a perfect storm that blows in when all you think you need is calm." He takes another sip from the glass. "She's beautiful chaos."

He's as far gone for this woman as I am for Katie.

"Have you told Gina that?" I question with a raised brow. "Does she know how you feel?"

"No." He finishes what's left at the bottom of his glass.

"Why not?" I realize the irony in my question as soon as I ask it. I'm the coward who couldn't tell Katie how I really felt before I broke her heart.

I wanted her and I wanted my daughter.

If I had spoken those words five years ago, I might not have lost all this time with her.

"She's my best friend's little sister." He pushes the glass at me. "She's forbidden fruit."

Katie's brother was never my best friend, but we had a bond, so I give this guy the best advice I can.

"Tell her how you feel." I scrub a hand over the back of my neck. "You can't know how the chips will fall until you're dealt the hand. Her brother may surprise you."

"He may kill me." He tugs a wallet from the inner pocket of his suit jacket. Two hundred dollar bills hit the top of the bar. "Thanks for the advice, Gage."

I pop a brow, surprised that he knows my name.

His offers his hand to me. "My dad used to own this place. I'm Daniel Lawton."

The pieces fall together at the mention of his name. He's Marlin Lawton's son. Marlin owned Lawtons before I bought it from his estate and rebranded it as the Tin Anchor.

I take his hand for a hearty shake. "I've heard great things about your dad from his regulars."

"Believe every word." He stands and straightens his gray suit jacket. "One of the last things he said to me was to grab hold of Gina before she slips away for good."

"He was a smart man," I say as my phone chimes.

He smiles. "He'd be glad you're running the ship now. Your advice is right on par with his."

It's a compliment I welcome.

"Get back to your girl." He motions to my phone. "I've got a lot to think about."

I take the few steps to my phone and glance down at the screen.

Kate: *Dinner tomorrow?*

I'll take it.

Gage: *Shrimp scampi works for you?*

Her response is quick and expected.

Kate: It works.

Gage: I'll see you at 7.

I punch out a text to Zeke telling him that he's got tonight to himself because tomorrow I need him.

I don't care if he can't make the switch. I'll close the bar down if I have to. I'm not missing a chance to cook Katie dinner.

Chapter 35

Kate

Silence is a mother's worst nightmare.

My mom would say that to me when I was a teenager hiding in my bedroom while I daydreamed about the captain of my high school's football team.

She started repeating the phrase right after I moved to Manhattan when I'd go days without calling her.

She left me a voicemail today. She only said those six words before she hung up.

I'm on the phone with her now.

"Is it a boy, Kate? Is that what's got your attention?"

I look through the dresses in my closet trying to decide which one to wear to Gage's apartment.

Maybe a dress is too formal and I should keep it casual in jeans and a blouse.

I sigh. "I date men, Mom, not boys."

"Of course." She laughs. "They're boys to me, Kate. If they're young enough to be my son, I consider them a boy."

Gage is not a boy.

"Are you busy at the store?" She effortlessly shifts the topic of discussion. "You're still selling enough dresses to keep the doors open, aren't you?"

"More than enough." I smile as I answer.

My parents doubted whether I could run the store on my own after I bought it.

They gifted both Eldred and me with a generous amount of money after my mom's dad passed away. I used the bulk of mine to fund my business.

I purchased the store's inventory from my former boss, signed a new lease deal with the building's landlord, and hired a contractor to handle the remodeling.

I've kept my head above water since.

"We're very proud of you," she says quietly. "Is anything else going on that I should know about?"

If I bring up Gage, she'll launch a defensive attack about why she never told me that he reached out to her and my dad after our broken engagement.

I don't have the time or the inclination to get into that with her tonight.

Gage is expecting me to be at his place in less than an hour.

"I need to run, mom," I chirp back, trying to keep my tone light to mask the nerves racing through me. "I'll talk to you in a day or two."

"Or seven?" She laughs. "I know you too well. You're off to meet a man."

"Mom," I say with an exaggerated bite of frustration in my voice. "I have to go."

"Fine, dear." She sighs. "I'll call you the day after tomorrow. Try to pick up."

"Bye, Mom." I yank my favorite little black dress from its hanger.

She exhales softly. "I'll keep my fingers crossed that the next time we talk you'll tell me you found the one and you're in love, Kate."

I grip the phone in my hand as the call ends.

Knowing she can't hear me, I say aloud what I've been too scared to admit to myself, "I did find the one eight years ago and I think I'm still in love with him."

***

A little more than an hour later, Gage flashes me a smile when he sees what I have in my hand.

I look past him to where a bottle of the same red wine is sitting on his coffee table.

I laugh. "Is this a case of great minds thinking alike?"

He takes the bottle from me. "You don't still drink this, do you?"

I take in how relaxed he looks in a white long sleeve sweater and blue jeans.

His feet are bare. His hair is neatly combed. It's a sharp contrast to the light growth of beard on his jaw.

Unlike the inexpensive wine we used to drink, Gage has only gotten better with age.

He closes his apartment door behind me, motioning for me to take a seat on his sofa.

"I haven't bought a bottle in years." I cross the apartment to the living room. "The last time was back in California."

It was three weeks before my life collapsed. I'd stopped on my way home and picked up a bottle so we could celebrate the fact that we were almost man and wife.

I remember that night vividly.

Our toast to our future was followed by a short discussion about kids.

Gage asked one last time if I was sure I'd never change my mind about being a mom. I told him I was one hundred percent certain.

Less than a month later he found out he was a dad.

"I'll check on dinner and crack this open." He holds up the wine bottle. "Or should I say I'll unscrew the cap?"

I drop my purse on the coffee table before I take a seat, nervously crossing my legs.

I sense his gaze on me, so I look up into his green eyes. I see familiarity there and promise.

"You being here means the world to me, Katie. Thank you for coming."

I glance down because the intensity in his eyes is too much.

"Don't move a muscle. I'll be right back." He walks away, leaving me to wonder what tonight holds.

Chapter 36

Gage

I'd say this feels like old times, but it doesn't.

The woman sitting on my sofa has been to hell and back on a ticket bought and paid for by me.

I destroyed her heart five years ago.

I can't even begin to imagine the full impact that my decision to leave had on her.

Yet, here she is.

She's open to more. I sense it in her kiss and the way she looks at me.

I open the bottle of wine and pour the deep red liquid into the only two wine glasses I own.

I live with few things.

The bulk of the furniture in here came with the place.

I have half of a closet of clothes, a few pairs of shoes, and a dozen or so pictures of my daughter.

Two are hanging in frames in the hallway. There's another on the wall in my bedroom. It's of the two of us. Kristin is sitting in my lap, looking up at me.

I stand in front of that picture and pray to the heavens above on a daily basis. My plea is always the same. I want time with my daughter. I want a chance to watch her grow up. I want her to fall asleep in the second bedroom down the hall.

I didn't bother placing any of the framed photos in the living room. I'm rarely in there. Most of my time at night is spent asleep or at the bar.

I fill daylight hours working out, doing administrative work at Tin Anchor or stuck in the armchair in my bedroom reading books.

It's a quiet existence. I see it as a bridge to what I really want.

A month ago that bridge took me to a future where I could see my daughter whenever I want. That's changed since I walked into Katie Rose Bridal.

I have no fucking idea if my life here is going to be uprooted and replanted in London, but I do know that I need to consider Katie in all of this.

It's presumptuous, but I sense that she's feeling something for me that mirrors what was in her heart before I broke up with her.

"Are you burning the shrimp scampi again?" Katie asks from where she's sitting on my sofa.

I glance over at her. She's peering over her shoulder at me. Her long hair is tumbling down her back.

She's a vision; a picture of innocence and bravery.

The most beautiful woman alive is what I see when I look at her.

"I burned it once." I laugh. "I would have thought you forgot about that by now."

She smiles. "I haven't forgotten anything, Gage."

Neither have I.

I remember everything including the way she mewls when I suck on her clit and the claw of her fingernails down my back when I'm driving my dick into her.

I want that tonight.

I need it.

I hope to hell that she wants it too.

***

She stopped herself after half a glass of wine.

I admit I was grateful. I wasn't looking for a repeat of the other night when the martinis melted her common sense.

I know if she would have been stone cold sober that night that I wouldn't have made it past the doorman of her building.

I want to win her over on a level playing field. I don't need the advantage that alcohol brings.

"I liked the dinner," she admits. "You can still cook shrimp scampi."

I mastered a few meals back in California.

I upped my kitchen game in Nashville when I became a dad.

The nights I had Kristin, I'd cook for her. The kid may have requested macaroni and cheese at every turn, but I broadened her culinary horizon.

By the time she was seven-years-old, seafood topped her request list followed by an array of vegetarian dishes.

One of the things I miss most about being shut out of my little girl's life is the moments spent in the kitchen cooking with her.

"Will Kristin be coming for a visit soon?" Katie's gaze shifts from my face to the half-full wine glass in front of her.

The woman is a mind reader.

She noticed me slipping into my thoughts. I'm not surprised that she instinctively knew that I was thinking about my daughter.

"I hope so."

I want her here in New York so I can take her to the observation deck on the top of the Empire State Building and a matinee of a Broadway musical.

Visiting Manhattan is on Kristin's bucket list.

It's well below meeting her favorite musician and getting a tattoo, but there are only so many dreams a dad can make come true.

"I'd like to meet her," Katie says quietly. "I like kids a lot."

I pop a brow. "I saw that when you were holding your friend's baby."

She lets out a sigh. "I love Arleth. I could hold her for hours."

"She looked peaceful in your arms."

Katie's hand moves to the back of her neck. "We've both changed a lot since we broke up."

I know where this is heading, so I don't stop her. I let her say what she needs to say.

"I think about being a mom." Her voice catches in her throat. I watch her swallow past something. I'd call it nerves since I witnessed firsthand the stress she was under in college and I've seen this reaction from her dozens of times. "Being a mom isn't what I thought it was."

"Olivia taught you differently?" I ask to lessen the weight that she's carrying.

She's trying to tell me that she's softened her stance on having kids. I'm not surprised. Time changes a person. It sure as hell changed me.

"Do you like being a dad?" She shifts the focus to me. I'll gladly grab the baton if it helps her ease into whatever she's feeling.

"I love it," I answer without a beat of hesitation. "It's everything."

Chapter 37

Kate

When I walk back into the living room, the table is cleared and Gage is sitting on the sofa.

I took longer than I wanted to in the bathroom.

I didn't have to do anything other than to splash cold water on my face and catch my breath.

Hearing him say that being a parent is everything filled me with a rush of emotions.

I excused myself and headed straight for the bathroom.

I used the time in there to think about the past and what the future might look like.

"Come sit with me, Katie," he says, turning to look at me.

He's lowered the lighting in the room and soft music is streaming from a small speaker on the coffee table.

It's the same mood he used to set before he'd bathe me.

Gage would draw me a candlelit bubble bath every Sunday after he cooked dinner for me. Sometimes he'd pour me a glass of wine or a tumbler filled with my favorite diet soda.

Every week he'd have a book of poetry in his hands as our favorite songs played from his phone.

He'd sit on the floor next to the claw foot tub while I soaked in the warm water.

The candle never cast enough light to read by so I knew that the poetry pouring from his lips came straight from his memory.

Yet, he'd flip through the pages, asking which poem I wanted to hear next.

After the bath, he'd dry me, take me to bed and fuck me until I couldn't breathe.

We'd fall asleep wrapped in each other's arms.

I take a seat next to him, taking care to leave some distance between us.

His gaze falls to my legs. "Your scar has faded."

I glance down at the jagged line on my skin. It's difficult to see in the dim light, but I know exactly where it is. Gage does too.

"Time heals all wounds," I quip, falling back on a piece of my mom's sage advice.

His gaze trails up my body to my face. "Does it?"

A month ago I would have said it didn't, but I can't anymore, so I don't. "I think it can."

His hands run up and down his muscular thighs. "Has it healed your wounds? The wounds I caused?"

"I wish you would have told me," I say quietly. "You should have told me about Kristin when you found out."

"I should have," he agrees with a nod of his chin. "I didn't think it through. If I could turn back the clock, I would have told you everything that day."

He can't turn back time. I can't either.

"I regretted it almost immediately," he confesses, scrubbing his hand over his forehead. "I've regretted it every minute of every day since."

"It's the past now." I sigh. "We can't go back and rewrite history."

His gaze scans my face. "You're right."

Our eyes lock and for the briefest moment I consider telling Gage a secret I've been carrying with me for years.

When we lived together, I was an open book. I told him everything knowing that he would accept all of my truths.

"Dance with me, Katie." He holds out his hand as a Frank Sinatra tune fills the air. "You used to love this song."

I slide my palm against his and let him pull me to my feet. "I still love this song."

"I still love you," he whispers so softly that I can barely make it out.

"Me too," I want to say back, but I don't.

He guides me to a small area next to the sofa. Taking me in his arms, he rests his hand on my back and tugs me close as we sway to the music and the very first song we ever danced to almost eight years ago.

***

I don't stop him when his hand glides down my back. It lands just above my ass. I move closer to him, knowing that's what he wants.

It's what I want too.

I didn't come here thinking that I'd sleep with my ex-fiancé, but it's the only thing I can focus on right now.

We've danced to seven or eight songs. I lost count after the third. Most of them had a much higher tempo than the Sinatra song, but we haven't stopped our slow dance.

He presses his cheek against mine. His voice comes out in a low growl. "I've missed you so much."

Emotion wraps itself around my heart. It squeezes until a breathless sound comes out of me.

He inches back to look in my eyes. "Have I told you that you're even more beautiful now?"

I shake my head. A smile that blooms from somewhere deep inside of me floats over my lips. "No."

"You are." His gaze drops to my mouth. "You're breathtaking."

He is too. The Gage who left five years ago was gorgeous with a mop of hair and a lean body, but now I'm looking at a striking, muscular, hot-as-hell man.

It could be confidence or maturity or maybe time has sculpted him into who he is today.

"I'm going to kiss you," he growls. "You want that."

He's not asking, but I don't care.

He knows I want to kiss him. He must know that I want more.

His lips meet mine in a slow, deep kiss.

Any hesitation I might have brought with me tonight melts under the brush of his tongue against mine and the taste of his breath.

He breaks the kiss. "I want you, Katie."

I look into the same green eyes that I stared into when he broke through my virginity under a bite of pain. They are the eyes that held fast to mine when I had my first orgasm with him deep inside of me.

My home is in those eyes.

"I want you," I whisper back before I press my lips to his again.

Chapter 38

Kate

I follow Gage without question when he takes my hand and guides me down the hallway.

I've wanted this since he walked back into my life, even if the desire was buried beneath a mountain of anger and grief.

Just as we enter his bedroom, he turns to me. His gaze searches my face for something. I know what it is. He wants reassurance that I'm ready.

He looked at me the same way the first time we made love.

I wasn't as nervous back then as I am now.

"Are you sure?" he asks, the rasp in his voice touching every part of me. "If you're not ready…"

Darting up to my tiptoes, I cup the back of his head so I can kiss him.

His hands circle me, tugging on my hips until I'm against him. The steely girth of his erection presses into me.

I break the kiss, dropping my hands to the front of his sweater.

"Take this off," I whisper. "Let me see you."

He nods before he tugs the sweater over his head, tossing it onto a chair in the corner.

A streetlight outside floods the room with a soft glow.

I stare at his body.

Everything is the same, yet it's different.

His chest is smooth. Tattoos or scars have never touched his skin.

The freckles I remember dot his upper chest. The trail of hair that leads to the waistband of his jeans is just as tempting as it was when I first saw it.

"It's your turn," he says, fisting his hands at his side.

I know Gage. I know that's how he tries to temper his need for me.

When we lived together, I'd make him wait while I'd dance around him naked, telling him that I wanted to see him hard before I'd let him touch me.

He would always laugh and point at his cock.

I know he's as hard in his jeans as he was every time I teased him.

"I'll help," he offers, circling his finger in the air.

I spin on my heel, bunching my hair into my hand. I hold it to the side, giving him access to the zipper that I struggled to do up at home when I was getting dressed.

I shiver when he grabs the zipper pull.

"I'll be gentle," he whispers into my ear, his breath racing over my skin.

I close my eyes when I feel the zipper open. I don't turn because I want him to slide the dress from my shoulders.

"Katie," he says my name in a rush as my dress falls to the floor. "You're so fucking beautiful."

I soak in the power of those words and the depth of need in his voice.

"Turn around," he urges with a hand on my hip. "Let me see you."

174

I move slowly, spinning back until I'm facing him. My hands fall to the lace waistband of my black panties.

He rakes me, stopping to stare at the matching black bra before his gaze settles on my hands. "Jesus, Katie. You're incredible."

Tears prick at the corner of my eyes. I'm not sad. I'm happy. I'm happier than I've been in five years.

I've belonged in this man's gaze, in his arms, and his bed.

"Don't cry." He takes a step closer to me, his hand darting to my cheek. "Please, Katie, don't cry."

I manage a smile that parts my lips. Trying to speak feels impossible at the moment. My voice is lost under what I want.

I want him. I want to touch him, and kiss him. I want to feel him inside of me.

I want to come around his cock, and against his lips.

I want everything.

His hands jump from my body to his. His eyes stay trained on mine as he unzips his jeans and pushes them to the floor along with his boxer briefs.

I reach down and undo the front clasp of my bra. Sliding it from my shoulders, I keep my eyes on his.

Before I can move to take my panties off, he's on me. His hands circle me, his lips find mine and he spins me around. He lowers me onto his bed until I feel the softness of a blanket on my back and the weight of his body on mine.

***

My breath catches somewhere in my chest when he slides the panties from me.

A low growl escapes him. "You're so fucking beautiful."

I close my eyes to ward off more tears. I'm overcome with a thousand different emotions. They're all too strong to contain.

The lash of his tongue over my smooth cleft draws my ass from the bed.

He pins me down, both hands holding my hips in place. "I need this, Katie. I need this so much."

I let go, feeling everything as if it's the first time.

He sucks my clit between his lips, biting it softly before he strokes it with the tip of his tongue, over and over again, just the way I want.

One hand glides down my body until his fingers touch the most sensitive part of me.

He knows what I like. Gage knows what will bring me to the edge, so he takes me there.

He slides one of his thick fingers into me as he gives my clit all the attention it craves.

I feel the burn of the approaching climax at the base of my spine, so I moan.

I moan so loudly that he stops briefly to lick the entire seam of my pussy before he brushes his tongue against my clit sending me into the clutches of an ear-shattering orgasm.

Chapter 39

Gage

I fumble with the condom package like I'm a first timer.

I might as well be. I haven't touched a rubber in a long time. Katie and I relied on her birth control after our first few months together.

We were both clean, so we felt safe.

The first time I was inside of her without a sheath around my dick, I came fast. It was fucking embarrassing.

I remember the way her cheeks flooded with pink when she felt me pump every last drop into her.

I came again, five minutes later as I watched her touch herself. She was wet from both of us.

The second time, I got on my knees, pulled her close and came down her throat.

I rip open the package and slide the condom on.

My back is to her. I can hear her breathing. She came hard when I had my face between her legs.

I needed more so I licked her to another orgasm, urging her on with my fingers and tongue.

The second time was quieter but more intense.

She shook beneath me, her hips bucked and she held fast to my head.

My lips are coated with her taste.

I lick them again, savoring it. It's tangy and sweet. It's everything I remember and more.

"Gage," she whispers. "Are you all right?"

I'm trying to find the will not to blow my load the minute I'm inside her pussy.

I turn to face her and it almost drops me to my knees.

She's on her back. Her long blonde hair is framing her perfect face. Her tits are full with hard pink nipples and every inch of her tall frame is smooth. She's glowing.

I close the distance between us with heavy steps until I'm on the bed, crawling over her.

She giggles when my sheathed cock brushes against her hip.

"You're as big as I remember," she gasps. "You're the biggest..."

I quiet her with a demanding kiss on the mouth. I don't want to know anything about the men who have fucked her.

I want to erase them from her memory.

I plan on doing that now.

I inch her legs apart, staring down at her body. I slide the tip in, savoring how it feels. "You're so sweet, Katie. Your pussy is so sweet."

A deep moan floats out from between her lips. "You remember."

I remember how I'd talk to her while I fucked her. I'd tell her how good she felt. How deep I'd go. I'd whisper in her ear that she was tight and wet.

I push in with a thrust, groaning when I'm buried deep within her.

She grabs my biceps, her nails raking my skin. "It's so much."

It's not enough.

I fuck her softly like this, so I can look into those hazel eyes, taking her to the edge with even strokes.

My restraint breaks when she wiggles beneath me trying to pull me closer. I take a kiss before her mouth is on my shoulder and her teeth break the skin.

I growl at her. A deep-seated need to take more consumes me, so I flip her over, grab her hips and fuck her with reckless abandon until we both come.

***

If I'm dreaming, I pray I never wake up.

I fell asleep after I tied off the condom, tossed it in the trash, and got in bed next to Katie.

My hand fumbles for my cock. I tangle my fingers in her long hair, guiding the pace as she sucks on my dick.

Jesus, this woman knows what the hell she's doing.

My eyes bolt open as reality sets in.

My Katie is giving me the best head I've ever had.

I look down at the top of her head as it bobs up and down. Her tongue is sliding along the thick vein that runs down the side. Her hand is squeezing the base, urging me on.

I fuck her mouth slowly, pushing my dick past the point where she used to gag.

She effortlessly swallows me.

It's too good.

It pisses me the hell off.

I twist her hair in my hands, angry that she's mastered sucking cock since we were together.

I press my eyes closed, trying to chase off the regret that's washing over me.

I fuck her mouth, drawing a sound from deep within her.

I don't stop.

"Tap my thigh if you want out," I spit out between clenched teeth. "If you don't, you're going to swallow it all."

She nods and sucks harder.

I throw my head back into the pillow and thrust up into her mouth over and over until I deliver on my promise.

Holding her in place, I come down her throat with a heady cry of her name.

Chapter 40

Kate

I know what's bothering him.

I've been watching Gage since I woke up. He was awake before me, sitting in a chair in his bedroom reading a book.

It's a mystery that I checked out of the library and read more than a year ago.

"Spoiler alert," I call out to get his attention.

He tilts up his chin to look at me, a broad smile taking over his mouth. "Spoiler alert?"

"The Colonel did it. It was in the library with a wrench."

He laughs, dropping his head back onto the chair. "You were always better at board games than I was."

"I read that book." I tug the blanket higher, shielding my nude body. "I do know the ending."

"Keep it to yourself." He drops the book on a small table next to the chair. "I'm two chapters away from finding out."

"I can give you a hint," I tease. "It's not who you think it is."

"How do you know who I think it is?" he questions back, a sly grin on his mouth.

"I know how your mind works."

He contemplates that, studying me from where he's sitting. "You always did."

I wish that were true. If I had that much insight into his thoughts, I might have been able to see what he was going through the day he broke off our engagement.

I'm tempted to bring up what I know he's feeling.

When we were having sex, I almost blurted out that he has the biggest cock of any man I've ever slept with. I don't know where the urge to say it came from, but I'm glad he stopped me.

I could feel the shift in him when I took him in my mouth.

He was asleep and I was craving the taste of him, so I slid down his body and circled the head of his dick with my lips.

His touch was tender at first, but when I took him deep, it shifted.

He was rough and demanding.

In the moment, it spurred me on more. I wanted to please him. I wanted him to feel the same pleasure he'd given me earlier.

Once it was over and I'd swallowed his release, I watched him get up from the bed.

I saw the way his shoulders tensed and his hands scrubbed his face.

He knows that I've had experiences since we've been apart.

I've been with men.

I've chased after the same feeling I had when I was in bed with Gage, but I couldn't find it until now.

I take in a deep breath and shake away the urge to delve into a deep conversation. "What time is it?"

He pushes to stand. He's wearing a pair of black boxer briefs. I can see the outline of his erection. He's aroused. I am too, but I need to get to my store.

"Does it matter?" He runs a hand down his chest to his stomach.

"I have to get to work," I say on a sigh.

"You can't be a little late?" His fingers trail along the waistband of his boxers. "Let me have you one last time before you leave."

Picking up his phone from the nightstand I glance at the time. "I have a shipment arriving in an hour, so I guess if you make it quick…"

"All I need is enough time to make you come," he growls. "Sit on my face. Ride me until you scream."

I'm on top of him the second he's on his back.

I lower myself onto his face. Closing my eyes, I get lost in all of it; his tongue, his lips, his teeth and the sounds he makes as he eats me.

Chapter 41

Gage

"The smile on your face is brighter than the sun."

I flash Gus an even wider grin. "Today's a good day."

"Every day is a good day," he comments, lowering onto the bench that faces the East River. "Life is what you make of it."

I can't disagree. "You're a wise man."

"You're a happy man." He points at me. "Tell me why that is."

"Katie," I say without hesitation. "She makes me happy."

"As happy as my Lois made me." He taps a finger on his chest. "I remember what it felt like to smile about a woman that way."

I glance out at the river. "We're in a good place, Katie and I."

"You can't ask for more than that." His voice softens. "Although most of us do. We don't realize how good we have it until it's all gone."

I turn to face him, raking a hand through my hair.

I took off for a run after Katie got dressed and rushed out of my apartment.

Her cheeks were still flushed from her orgasm. Her hair was a mess. She gave me a quick kiss before she was out the door.

Just as I was about to hit the shower, I realized that I smelled like her.

I wanted that to linger, so I put on a pair of black running shorts and hit the pavement.

"Maybe one day you'll bring her around here?" Gus asks with a perk of his graying brow. "I'd love to meet the girl who stole your heart."

"Maybe one day," I offer back.

I'm too selfish to consider that at the moment. I don't want to share Katie's attention with anyone.

I just got her back. If I had my way, we'd lock ourselves in my apartment for a month, but that's not reality.

There are still things I need to say to her. I have truths that I need to reveal.

I'll fight like hell to make certain that nothing gets in the way of what we're rebuilding, but life has a way of tossing a curveball into the mix.

"I'm going to sit with my thoughts for a minute." Gus shoots me a look.

I know a subtle push-off when I hear it. I take the hint respectfully, as I always do. "I'll leave you to that."

"I'll see you and Katie soon, will I?"

"I can't promise when you'll meet Katie, but I'll be around."

"I suppose that's something to look forward to." He winks. "Make today the best you can, Gage. Tomorrow isn't promised to anyone."

***

An hour later, I'm standing at the front entrance to Katie Rose Bridal with a blueberry muffin in one hand and a cup of Earl Grey tea in the other.

I rap on the door again, willing Katie to hear me before this tea burns a hole right through the goddamn paper cup.

The barista asked if I wanted it iced or hot. I said hot and he fucking delivered.

I see a flash of someone moving in the boutique.

Natalie appears behind the glass with a smile on her lips.

She unlocks the door and swings it open. "Gage? What are you doing here so early?"

It's almost nine. Katie left my place more than an hour-and-a-half ago.

"I'm here to see Katie." I push my way past her. "She didn't have time for breakfast this morning."

"You know this because…" her voice trails as she locks the door behind me.

I ignore the question she didn't ask. "Point me in Katie's direction before this tea burns a hole through my hand."

She reaches for the cup.

I don't stop her because my hand comes in handy when I'm behind the bar at Tin Anchor.

She rests the cup on the reception counter, taking time to slide a piece of paper underneath it so it won't damage the wood. "Kate's not here."

"She's not?"

"No." She faces me. "Did she tell you that she'd be here?"

I'm not fueling the fire that is this woman's curiosity. If she wants answers about where Katie and I stand, those need to come from the woman I love.

I won't fill in the blanks for Natalie.

"Where is she?" I rest the muffin and the napkin it's wrapped in on the counter next to the tea.

"She came in to take care of a delivery, but she took off right after." She peels back one layer of the napkin to have a look. "You got this from the bakery around the corner, didn't you? No one else in the five boroughs can make a muffin this good."

I'm not in the mood to talk about the superiority of one baked good over another.

"I can call her and tell her that you're here," she offers. "Although I should warn you that I tried calling her right before you banged on the door, but she didn't pick up."

"I'll track her down." I slide my phone from the front pocket of my jeans.

"Are you taking these with you?" Natalie's hand floats over the tea and treat.

I huff out a laugh. "Consider those yours, Nat."

"A tea, a blueberry muffin, and a nickname?" She reaches for the tea. "You're a keeper. I hope Kate has figured that out."

I hope she has to.

Chapter 42

Kate

I took a *Kate-day* today.

My mom coined the phrase when I was struggling with an assignment in high school. She knew that I was beating my head against the wall, in a non-literal sense, so she proposed that I skip school for the day so I could hang out with her.

We started at her favorite spa.

I had my first manicure and pedicure that day.

Our next stop was the mall. I spent some of the money I'd saved from working at a candy store after school twice a week.

I bought a pair of ripped jeans and a sweatshirt.

Lunch was my mom's treat. We had steak sandwiches and red velvet cake for dessert.

That was one of the best Kate-days I ever had.

Today's version was more subdued.

I went to the library to return two poetry books I'd loaned out. After that, I dropped in to see my favorite hair stylist. She fit me in for a quick trim.

Crispy Biscuit was my next stop. Usually, I'm there with Tilly or Olivia for brunch, but today I ate lunch alone at my favorite diner.

I've spent the last two hours on a bench in Central Park watching the faces of the city pass me by.

Today's Kate-day had no rhyme or reason to it.

It was simply a few hours with my phone turned off and my mind racing.

I couldn't stop thinking about Gage. Every thought about last night was balanced with a memory from five years ago.

I want a new beginning with him, but the past feels like it's watching from somewhere in the darkness waiting to leap out to steal the future away from me again.

What if we can't make this work?

What if he moves to London to be closer to his daughter?

What if he can't look at me the same way after he learns my secret?

I press the home button on my phone to power it back up. On a typical Kate-day, no one notices that I've checked out of my daily life for a few hours.

Today is different.

I scan the screen of my phone as it chimes, buzzes and even rings reminders of all the messages and calls I've missed.

Three of the text messages are from Natalie. They can wait. The issues she asked about would have been resolved by now since it's been hours since she texted me.

My mom called twice and left one voicemail. I don't listen to it. I'll save it for tonight when I have time to sit through a ten minute recounting of the yoga class she had this morning.

Her bi-monthly trek to the yoga studio a few blocks from her house is always followed by a call to me to describe the new poses she's learned.

I skim through the rest of my text messages.

One is from Tilly about dinner later this week. Olivia sent one to tell me that Arleth finally mastered rolling over. I open the video clip she attached.

Joy tugs at my heart as I watch the little girl wiggle her hips before she slowly rolls over. The sound of Olivia cheering her on in the background brings a smile to my face.

I scroll back to the notifications.

Gage called twice, but he didn't leave a voicemail.

I see why when I read the string of text messages from him.

The first is simple and straightforward.

Gage: *I'm looking for you. I just left your store.*

I check the time on that one. It was shortly after nine this morning. I had been at the boutique but left after a delivery arrived.

The second message was an hour later.

Gage: *Look up at the sun. It's got nothing on you. Your smile is brighter and better.*

I laugh aloud. Whenever he took me out on his parents' sailboat he'd say that to me. The first time I heard the compliment, I accused him of trying to charm his way into my bikini bottoms. He laughed and winked. The second time he said it, my bikini hit the deck as soon as we were in open water and out of view.

I glance up at the late afternoon sun before my gaze drops back to my phone and the last message he sent.

Gage: *Today is Kate-day, isn't it? I hope it's everything you need it to be.*

With tears clouding my vision, I read the last two lines of his text in a whisper, "He knew where she was without a word from her lips. She lived in his heart; today and forevermore."

Chapter 43

Kate

Two hours later, I walk into Tin Anchor with a red dress on and a poetry book in my hand.

After I got home from Central Park, I pulled a cardboard box out of my bedroom closet. I stared at it for at least ten minutes before I opened it and tossed all the contents onto my bed.

Most of it was my collection of winter accessories. The countless pairs of knitted mittens and scarves are courtesy of my mom.

I have at least one set in every color of the rainbow.

Hidden beneath that treasure trove was the item I needed to see.

It's the poetry book that I'm clinging to now.

It was the last gift that Gage ever gave to me. It was wrapped in newspaper and a pink ribbon when he put it in my hands.

My favorite poet, Grayson Marks, inscribed the book to me. Crying, I thumbed through it noting right away that Gage had dog-eared a page. On it was a poem and a circle of red ink.

Inside the circle were two simple lines.

He knew where she was without a word from her lips. She lived in his heart; today and forevermore.

Gage told me to always remember that I would live in his heart until the day he died and that if he closed his eyes, he'd feel me with him.

Just a few months later, he set sail without me and everything changed.

I approach the bar, hoping that he'll be finished with the male customer by the time I reach him.

I have a million things to say, but only four words have been playing on the tip of my tongue since I read his last text. It's the words I haven't said to him since the day before he left me.

I love you, Gage.

He spots me as I near him. The serious look on his face softening into something I've seen countless times.

It's love, compassion, kindness, and a heavy dose of lust.

He always loved me in red.

He used to tell me that it was a reflection of the spark that's inside of me.

I watch as he smiles at the man before he moves to the side.

"Katie." My name leaves him in a low growl as soon as I'm standing next to an empty stool across the bar from him. "Red is your color."

"You love me in red," I say softly. "You used to tell me that."

"It captures your fire." His gaze drops to my hand. "Is that…"

"The book you gave me." With a shaking hand, I rest it on the bar. "You remembered the passage."

With a heavy swallow, he exhales. "I didn't think you kept anything. It wasn't in the box of things you left behind in our apartment, so I thought you trashed it."

"I couldn't," I admit, taking a seat on the stool. "I packed it away. I brought it to New York with me."

His eyes catch mine. "I'm glad. I'm really glad."

"Did I live in your heart, Gage?" I ask, my bottom lip trembling. "Did you think about me after you left?"

His hands find mine. He scoops them into his, calming them instantly with his touch. "You always lived in my heart. I thought about you endlessly. A day didn't pass where I didn't wake up with you on my mind."

He was never far from my thoughts either.

I may have fooled myself into believing that I could forge a life without him, but if I'm being honest, I longed for his touch every minute of every day.

"I love you, Katie."

I stare at his lips, soaking in the depth of those words.

He used to say them to me at least a dozen times a day, but never before have they pierced my heart the way they are now.

I'm aching to repeat them back to him, but there's something I need to tell him first. I'm not brave enough to do it today. I want a little more time to bask in the knowledge that he still loves me.

"Should we take this to my place?" he asks with a perk of his right brow. "Zeke can cover for me."

I nod without saying a thing.

All I want tonight is to be in his bed. I hope with everything I am that when I wake in his arms tomorrow that courage will have found its way to me.

***

Gage lets out a deep sigh. "You have the most perfect ass. How in the hell is it this perfect?"

Glancing at him, I laugh. "Your ass isn't half-bad either."

All of him is chiseled perfection.

I watched him undress in the daylight. We used to make love with the lights on back in California. Dusk hasn't settled over Manhattan yet, so we've been enjoying the early evening light by exploring one another.

I'm on my stomach. My nude body is stretched out on Gage's bed. He's next to me, on his side, his stiff cock teasing me each time I steal a glance at it.

We've been at his apartment for almost an hour, but we haven't fucked yet.

Our hands have been on a quest to write to memory every inch of each other's skin.

His hand grazes over my ass again. "I could stare at this for hours."

I rest my cheek on my arm. "I can think of something else you can do for hours."

"Eat you?" His fingers dive between my cheeks, skimming lower until he touches my core. "Is that what you want? You want my mouth here?"

I part my legs slightly, granting him more access. "Your fingers."

A deep groan comes from somewhere inside of him as he skims two fingers over my pussy. "You want me to finger fuck you, Katie?"

I close my eyes. "Please."

He slides one finger into my channel. Within a second another joins it. It's not nearly as much as his thick cock, but it's enough to lure my hips off the bed.

"That's it," he whispers into my ear. "Fuck my fingers."

I easily find a rhythm, pushing up against his hand before I draw back down.

"Let go." His breath skims over my shoulder. "Fuck it until you're close."

I up my pace. Chasing my release, sweat beads on my forehead.

"Tell me how badly you want to come." His teeth graze the skin of my neck. "How much do you want it?"

"So much." I pant, not caring that I'm losing control from just the touch of his fingers.

"Touch your clit," he orders. "Lightly, Katie. Don't take yourself there yet."

I nod. My hand crawls down the blanket until it reaches my core. I moan aloud when my fingertips skim the swollen nub of nerves.

I hear the nightstand drawer open and the grunt that follows. He's sheathing his cock so he can drive it into me.

I apply more pressure. Making tighter circles, I moan as I race to the edge.

"Don't come," he says harshly. "You're going to come on my cock."

He flips me over, pins my hands to the bed above my head and pushes into me with one fierce thrust.

I come instantly, colors dancing behind my eyelids, my skin heating, and my heart exploding.

"Ah, fuck," he bites out before he pounds into me, sending me straight into the clutches of another climax.

Chapter 44

Gage

I wake to the image of Katie standing in my bedroom.

She's not watching me sleep. She's staring at the picture of Kristin and me. I don't know how much detail she can make out in the darkened room, but it's enough to keep her attention laser-focused on the photograph.

She chews on the nail of her right thumb.

I know exactly what that means. She has questions.

"You're awake," I croak out in a deeper than normal voice.

"You're sexy," she says quietly looking over at me.

I'd tell her the same thing, but sexy doesn't even begin to describe how she looks.

She's wearing a pair of red lace panties and nothing else.

I was always enamored with Katie's body. That hasn't changed. If anything, I'm more obsessed with her now than when I was twenty-four.

"Come back to bed." I pat the wrinkled sheet next to me.

"In a minute." Her gaze drops to the floor. "When's the last time you saw your daughter?"

The answer should be simple. I wish I could say that I saw her this afternoon or a week ago.

The reality is that it's been way too fucking long.

I push the sheet down and swing my legs over the side of the bed. I won't have this conversation when I'm naked.

"I'll make some coffee." I reach for the boxer briefs I kicked off before I climbed into bed.

I feel her gaze on me as I tug on the briefs and cross the room to my closet to grab a pair of black sweatpants.

"I should get dressed too," she says. "Where did my dress end up?"

It's in the living room. I stripped her bare right after we got here.

I tug a blue dress shirt from one of the hangers in my closet. "You can wear this."

She nods. "Is it alright if I meet you in the kitchen in a few minutes?"

I welcome the time alone. I need to figure out how the hell to tell her the secret I've been carrying with me since we reconnected.

Pressing a kiss to her mouth, I hand her the shirt and take off down the hallway, with my heart thundering inside my chest.

***

"Did I overstep when I asked about Kristin?"

I glance up from my half-empty coffee mug and study Katie's face. I see concern blanketing her expression.

I know why it's settled there. She thinks I'm torn up about the fact that I haven't seen my daughter recently.

She has no idea that it reaches well beyond that.

I shake my head. "No, not at all."

She takes another small sip of coffee. Her gaze wanders around the living room. We're sitting on the sofa. She gathered the blue wool throw she knit for me over her legs.

I love that she felt comfortable enough to do that.

Memories of nights in California spent on our sofa flit through my mind.

I was too trusting back then.

I took the word of an ex-girlfriend over the plea in the eyes of the woman I loved.

If I had told my fiancée that Madison claimed Kristin was mine, Katie would have kept a level head.

I know for a fact that she would have told me to get a DNA test.

I didn't cross that bridge until Perry, Madison's ex-lover and current husband, walked into the picture and I saw my daughter's chin, and her nose in his profile.

"Will you be seeing her soon?" Katie presses for more.

I can't blame her for wanting to know. I fucked off once because of my child. There has to be concern rooted deep within her that the same thing would happen all over again.

I rest my mug on the table and turn to face her.

I bite the fucking bullet because I'm done hiding behind my view of what I think Katie needs or wants to hear.

I give it to her straight knowing that the chips are about to fall where they may.

"I don't know when I'll see Kristin." I pause and draw in a deep breath. "I'm not her biological father."

Chapter 45

Kate

I'm speechless.

I've never met Kristin, but I've seen pictures of her. She has the same color eyes as Gage. Her brown hair is the same shade as his.

When I saw her smile in the first photograph he showed me, I swore that it was the spitting image of her father's smile.

Gage isn't her father.

At least not by blood, but the love he has for that little girl is evident in his voice when he talks about her and in his eyes now.

He can't mask the pain that he's in.

"I didn't question whether she was mine or not." He hangs his head in his hands. "I love her as much as I would a child that had my blood running through them."

Emotion knots my gut.

"Madison's ex came to Nashville looking for her a couple of years ago." His voice evens. "I didn't meet the guy right off, but months later I ran into him when he was leaving Madison's place one morning."

"He looks like Kristin?" I ask the obvious question.

"There's a resemblance." His hand scrubs his chin. "I shrugged it off at first, but it all came to a head one morning and the truth came out."

"What happened?"

"I asked Madison if there was a chance that I wasn't Kristin's dad." He finally glances in my direction. "She came to my apartment and confessed. She told me that she'd screwed him once days after our last time together. She did the math."

"She sucks at math," I say under my breath.

It lures a faint smile to his mouth. "She said he was her rebound. When she was found out she was pregnant, she assumed I was the dad."

"She didn't tell you for four years." I shrug my shoulders. "Why did she wait so long?"

"Our relationship ended badly." He closes his eyes briefly. "She said that she didn't want to subject a child to that bitterness."

She changed her tune as soon as she found out that Gage was set to marry me. It doesn't take a genius to figure that out.

"Madison stopped at my parents' house because her mother willed a necklace to my mom," he goes on, "from what I understand, my mom told her that she'd wear it to my wedding."

"She told you about Kristin once she knew that you were marrying me." My words sound petulant.

Madison made a choice, but Gage did as well.

He could have told me what was happening. I would have told him to take a step back and consider the possibility that the child wasn't his.

I admit that the drive to urge him to question Kristin's paternity would have been coming from a selfish place. I didn't want kids when I was on the cusp of becoming Gage's wife.

Despite that, I know that I would have accepted his daughter. I would have fallen in love with her as desperately as he did when he saw her beautiful face with those big green eyes and the crooked grin.

It might have taken me time to do that.

Not months, or years, but weeks.

A heart can heal when it's placed in tender hands.

My mom said that to me a month-and-a-half after I'd moved to Manhattan. She wanted to fix me up with the son of one of her friends. He lived in Boston but was headed to New York City for business.

I turned her down.

My heart was already in tender hands by then.

"I'm doing everything I can to see her." His voice quakes. "I won't stop until I can tell her face-to-face how much I love her."

"I'm sorry that Madison won't let that happen," I offer, fighting the urge to call his ex-girlfriend a bitch.

"Perry's threatened by my relationship with Kristin." His jaw clenches. "He petitioned the court to have his name added to her birth certificate. Madison hasn't admitted it, but I know he was behind my arrest when I tried to see Kristin in London."

He was arrested trying to see his daughter? What the hell?

How can any parent cut off contact with a person who raised their daughter? What is the reasoning behind removing a loving caregiver from a child's life?

"I'm sorry, love." The endearment leaves my lips before I realize what I've said.

I haven't called him *love* in forever.

Gage shifts until he's right next to me. His hand darts to my cheek. "You can't know what that does to me, Katie. Hearing you call me that."

I stare into his eyes. "I want to help. Tell me how I can help you see your daughter."

"We will see my daughter," he says assuredly. "I want you to meet her."

I want that too, more than I realized until this very moment.

"I should have explained about the complications with her custody the day I told you about her."

I quiet him with a soft kiss to the lips. I hold him against me, my breath melding with his.

As desperately as I want to confess my secret to him, I can't. Not now. Tonight I need to comfort him.

Chapter 46

Gage

I curse under my breath. I don't know what the fuck I was thinking when I agreed to host this bachelor party.

Katie is waiting for me at her apartment.

We made love early this morning after I told her that I wasn't Kristin's biological father.

It was Katie who urged me back into bed.

She dropped my shirt on the floor and wrapped her body around mine.

I was hard instantly.

After taking me in her mouth, she took me inside of her.

I was sheathed and wanting. I fucked her slowly, but the need to hear her come drove me to up the pace.

With wild, frantic fucks I took her over the edge before I emptied myself into the condom with long, heavy breaths.

She kissed me goodbye before she left for work and made me promise that once Myles's bachelor party was over, I'd be in her bed.

It's after midnight.

Cases of beer have been emptied. Money has exchanged hands at the pool table and the ball game that was blaring from the television was over hours ago.

I shut down Tin Anchor for this.

I won't lose time more time with Katie for it.

"You're itching to leave." Zeke elbows me. "Isn't the best man supposed to have more fun than the groom at a party like this?"

"I don't have a rule book." I pat the empty back pocket of my jeans. "I'm winging it."

"You've done good." He points a finger at Myles who is barely managing to keep himself upright on a chair. "He won't remember a thing tomorrow."

I laugh. "I wouldn't bet against you on that."

"What's his bride's name again?" Zeke runs the bar towel in his hand over a wineglass.

"Annalise."

"That's a far cry from Karen."

I know where this is headed. I heard Myles mention his ex once or twice tonight. I tried to get him back on track by talking about how excited Annalise is for the big day.

We're three weeks out from the wedding.

"If you did have that rule book," Zeke starts before he turns to face me. "On page nine, paragraph three you'd find that it's the best man's duty to have a talk with the groom about the ex he's still in love with before he takes a vow to honor another woman for eternity."

My brows pop up. "Is that so?"

"Would you want your sister marrying a guy who is hung up on someone else?"

"I don't have a sister," I point out a fact that Zeke knows all too well.

"I do," he counters. "I have two and I can tell you that I would step into the middle of it before any shit hit the fan."

"It's already hit, wouldn't you say?" I jerk a thumb in Myles's direction.

Zeke looks over to catch the groom-to-be sobbing over his empty beer glass.

I tug my phone out of my pocket so I can send Katie a text telling her I'm on my way soon. "I'll have a sit-down with Myles in a day or two. I can't stand next to him when he marries Annalise if Karen is still carting his heart around town."

Zeke pats my shoulder. "Myles knew what he was doing when he picked you to be his best man."

"Get him an Uber and a coffee to go." I pull up Katie's contact information even though I've got her number saved to memory. "Let's clear this place out. There's somewhere I need to be."

***

The beauty in this vision could drop me to my knees and keep me there for eternity.

Katie in a white tank top and white lace panties with a just woken glow about her is angelic.

I storm past her and slam the door to her apartment shut.

I take her in my arms. The warmth radiating from her body permeates my skin. The scent of her is intoxicating.

Jesus, I love this woman with every part of my soul.

"I fell asleep after you texted me," she whispers into my neck. "I was dreaming about you."

I walk backward down her hallway, tugging her along with me. "Tell me about that dream."

"We were on the sailboat." She sighs. "It was windy. Not crazy windy but just the right kind of windy. You know what I mean."

I know exactly what she means.

It's the warm wind that she always loved.

It would bathe her skin after we fucked on my parents' boat. She'd lie naked on her back while she floated down from the high of her orgasm.

I'll never forget those moments.

The world didn't exist. It was just the water, the sky and the two of us.

"What else do you remember about the dream?"

"He was there," she murmurs.

I stop dead in place. "Who?"

Her heavy-lidded eyes drift up to my face. "Who what?"

"You said he was there, Katie."

Her brows pinch together. "I did?"

There was only ever one *he* other than me in our relationship. Teddy, the cranky cat that Katie adopted from a woman in our building.

The cat couldn't fucking stand me, but it loved Katie.

She loved him just as fiercely.

When he died, she was inconsolable.

"You're talking about old Teddy, aren't you?" I stop when the back of my knees hit her bed. "You were dreaming about him being on the boat with us?"

"Teddy," she says his name on a sigh. "I miss him."

"I'll help you forget about him for tonight." I brush my lips over hers. "I'll give you something new to dream about."

Her gaze drops to my hands. "I think I'll like that dream if it involves you without any pants on."

My jeans slide to the floor, followed by my boxer briefs. My cock is painfully hard. "In that case, you're going to love that dream."

Chapter 47

Kate

Last night is a blur.

I fell asleep but was jarred awake by a text message from Gage telling me he'd be at my place within the hour.

I drifted off again after that so when he knocked on my apartment door, I stumbled to open it.

I told him about my dream.

I didn't mean to tell him about all of it.

Secrets will find a crack and they'll seep out eventually.

When my mom said that to me I was fourteen-years-old and a cheater. It wasn't a boy that I couldn't stay faithful to. It was my history teacher.

I stumbled on the answer key to a midterm quiz on his desk after school.

I stored to memory the first ten answers and then aced the fifteen-question test the next day.

My mistake was thinking that I'd gotten away with it.

A month later I thought I was home alone. My mom thought I was a straight-A student based on merit.

We were both wrong.

She was in the laundry room when she heard me humble bragging about the test to my best friend at the time.

I failed the class.

I haven't lied since, until now.

A lie of omission is still a lie.

I walk back into my bedroom and the sight of the man I love fast asleep in my bed.

Today is the day that I put my heart back in his hands.

Pieces are missing.

It's bruised and battered, but it belongs to him.

***

An hour later, he's finally awake.

I wish I could say it's because he sensed when I walked back into the bedroom to check on him, but that's not what woke him up.

It was the ringing of his phone.

It's in his hand now, pressed to his ear.

He's talking to a man named Dylan about Kristin.

I turn to leave the room because this conversation feels private. Gage's voice is low pitched and his gaze is pinned to the bed.

I walk back into the living room.

I showered and dressed while he was asleep.

I applied my makeup and made a pot of coffee.

The entire time I rehearsed what I need to say to Gage in my head. I ran over the words dozens of times, tweaking them until I finally settled on a mini-speech that I pray I can get through without falling apart.

"Katie."

I turn at the sound of Gage's voice. He's standing behind me, still dressed in only boxer briefs.

"Is everything all right?"

"Better than all right." He smiles broadly. "Madison put in a call to her attorney. She wants to talk directly to mine ASAP. I think I'm a step closer to seeing my daughter."

That's cause for celebration. I have orange juice and a cheap bottle of champagne that Tilly gave me so I could ring in the New Year while I watched the ball drop in Times Square on my television.

I wasn't in the mood to celebrate then. I'm not now.

I'm in the mood to confess.

"Is that coffee that I smell?" He turns toward my kitchen. "I'd give almost anything for a cup. Name your price."

Forgiveness. That's all I want.

"I'll get it." I move toward my small kitchen.

"Are you going in to work?" he asks from behind me. "It's not even eight a.m. and you look ready to face the day."

I'm not.

I'm not even sure I'm ready to face him, so I keep my back turned as I pour hot coffee into a ceramic mug.

I feel the brush of his hand on my shoulder just as I'm reaching for the sugar. "What's wrong? Something's not right."

Emotions war within me. Sadness clashes with anger. Fear battles with desperation.

Ultimately, grief wins.

Tears well in the corners of my eyes as I stare down at the countertop.

"I need to tell you something," I whisper.

"Tell me." Both of his hands are on my shoulders now. "Please, Katie."

I suck in a breath that's meant to strengthen my resolve to do this. I just need to get out four words to start with. They are words that I've never uttered aloud. I've carried them inside of me for so long that they've etched themselves into my soul.

Leaving the coffee mug on the counter, I turn to face Gage.

I have to be looking into his eyes when I say this. I need him to understand how profoundly my life was impacted five years ago.

I packed this pain into a box somewhere deep inside of me. That was the only way I could deal with it, but I can't ignore it anymore. Being with Gage again has opened it up and everything that I've kept hidden has surfaced.

"Whatever it is, you can tell me," he says as he studies my face. "Whatever it is, it's all right. I'm here. I'm not going anywhere."

I nod. Pulling every last shred of strength from within me, I grab his cheeks and cradle them in my hands. "Gage, I…"

The shrill bite of his phone ringing interrupts me.

His gaze drops to it and with it my heart plummets in my chest.

"Fuck," he says between clenched teeth. "It's my lawyer. Dylan. It's about Kristin. I have to take this, Katie. I'm sorry. I have to."

I turn back to the counter.

Tears stream down my cheeks as I listen to him tell the man on the other end of the call that he's leaving now to go see his daughter.

Chapter 48

Gage

I'm dressed and out the door of Katie's bedroom before I end the call to Dylan.

I can't believe that my daughter will be in my arms in less than twenty-four hours.

"Katie," I call out her name as I pocket my phone. "Where are you?"

"In the kitchen," she says in an even tone.

I round the corner and almost run right into her. I study her face. She's been crying. I don't have to ask why.

"You always cried whenever I got good news." I skim my fingers over her chin. "When I was accepted into medical school, I think you cried more tears of joy than I did."

Her lips part but she doesn't say anything.

I want her next to me when I see Kristin, but that's asking too much of her and too much of my daughter.

I want her to know Katie. Hell, I know Kristin is going to eventually love Katie as much as I do, but I have to pace this. They both need time to adjust to the presence of the other in my life.

"Kristin is on her way to Los Angeles."

Surprise draws her brows up. "I thought she was in London."

"I thought the same." I rub my jaw. "Madison is visiting family in L.A. and Kristin is with her. They're set to board a flight within the hour. I need to get home and pack. I'm heading back to California."

I kiss her hard. I can't contain everything I'm feeling. I want to head to the top of the Empire State Building so I can scream to the world that I've got my life back.

I fucking have everything I've wanted in my hands and I'm never letting go.

"I love you, Katie," I tell her so she knows that this time I'm coming back to her. "I'll be back in a few days."

"You'll be back," she repeats.

"I. Will. Come. Back," I say each word slowly and with purpose. "Nothing is going to keep me away from you."

Her eyes lock on mine.

I kiss her again, wrapping my arms around her. "I'll call you after I see Kristin."

I turn and march to the door of her apartment. Glancing over my shoulder, I see her standing next to the window staring up at the blue sky.

I can't wait to get back to her, but for now, I need to get my ass to California so I can hug my little girl.

***

"Daddy!"

I'm on my knees before Kristin reaches me. I don't give a shit that we're in the middle of a hotel lobby.

I've waited for this day for months.

216

I cradle her face in my hands, studying the light in her eyes and the smile on her face.

Her features have matured. She's at least an inch taller than she was the last time I saw her.

Madison cut off video messaging between us months ago before she axed text messages too.

I have less than two days to catch up on my little girl's life.

"I've missed you, Tin."

"Oh, Daddy." She kisses my cheek. "I've missed you so much. Mommy said I get to see you more."

I look up at Madison. I haven't given her a second glance since she waved me over after I walked into the hotel.

"Madison," I say her name curtly.

"Gage." She nods, her arms crossing her chest.

Nothing about her has changed. Her brown hair is still cut in a bob. Her blue eyes are tinged with sadness.

"How's Perry?" I ask without a hint of resentment.

I never wanted Kristin to be subjected to the bullshit around her.

I tried to keep things calm after I found out I wasn't her biological father. I didn't want anything to change, but Perry wanted the family he thought he deserved.

"Divorcing me," she quips, waving her bare left hand in the air.

"Daddy Perry is divorcing us." Kristin shrugs. "He found a new family, Daddy."

I raise a brow at Madison. "He what exactly?"

"Fell in love with his assistant." She pats her stomach. "She's having his baby. He calls it a new beginning. I call it an alimony check."

I toss her a look meant to silently tell her to shut the hell up.

Kristin doesn't need to hear that.

"We're going to look for a new house." Kristin wraps her arms around my neck. "You can live next door."

Tears prick the corners of my eyes.

This is exactly what I've wanted.

"Daddy has a new family now too."

I glance at Madison and the look I toss her this time is a clear, *what the fuck are you talking about*?

"Granny and Papa Burke met us at the airport." Madison smiles. "Your mom said that you were back with Kate Wesley."

My parents had to have been overjoyed to see Kristin. They missed being called Granny and Papa. They missed everything about her almost as much as I have.

When I called them before I left New York, I mentioned that I reconnected with Katie. I didn't expect a response from them, so I wasn't surprised when my dad changed the subject to the weather.

There was no offer from them to meet me when my flight landed.

"Is Katie your new family, Daddy?" Kristin nudges my face so she can look into my eyes. "Does she have a baby in her tummy too?"

"No baby." I kiss the tip of her nose. "Katie is my old friend. I want you to meet her."

"Slow down." Madison's hand jumps into the air. "One step at a time, Gage."

"Our first step is having dinner together." I give Kristin a big hug as I look at Madison. "We can take care of everything else after that."

Chapter 49

Kate

I stare down at my phone.

I haven't heard anything from Gage since yesterday.

He called me from Minneapolis. His connecting flight to L.A. was delayed by a few hours.

I was in the middle of a consult with a bride and her party of twelve friends and relatives.

All their voices drowned out Gage's.

I explained that I was busy. He understood, ending the call by telling me that he was excited to be a dad again.

I clutched the phone in my hand as I bit back the emotion that swept over me.

When I turned back to the face the soon-to-bride she mistook the tears in my eyes for approval of the gown she had on.

She bought it on the spot.

"What secrets does that thing hold?" Callie asks from behind the bar.

I'm at Tin Anchor.

I stopped in after work for a martini.

The need to feel close to Gage was strong so coming here seemed like the right thing to do.

"This thing?" I wave my phone in the air. "My mom calls it a stress magnet."

Callie laughs.

I expected her brother, Zeke, to be tending bar, but he's not in sight.

I only sat on this stool and introduced myself as a friend of Gage's ten minutes ago, but I already like her.

She's younger than me, but she's wise.

I listened to her offering advice to the man who was seated next to me. She told him to push his stubborn male pride aside and tell someone named Gina that he's crazy about her.

She tucks her dark brown hair behind her shoulders. "Your mom is right."

A laugh bubbles out of me. "What's it like working for Gage?"

Her blue eyes widen. "This is off the record, right?"

I nod. "I won't tell him anything."

"He's the best." She wipes the top of the bar with a towel. "He's been good to Zeke. He hired him first and when he heard that I needed a part-time job, he offered this to me on the spot. I pick and choose my hours. He pays well and we keep all of our tips."

"He's a good man," I say without any hesitation.

"Can I tell you something?"

I scratch the back of my hand; anxious that it will be something I don't want to hear. "Please."

"The first time he talked about you I thought to myself that I hoped that one day a man would love me that same way." Her lips curve up. "You're the luckiest woman in the world, Kate."

I don't ask her to repeat what Gage told her about me. I already know. I feel it when he touches me, and I hear it his voice.

I see it when I look up at the shelf behind the bar that holds the treasures of my past life with him.

"Does he have a brother?" she asks jokingly.

"Two happily married ones."

"Well, shit." She laughs. "I guess I have to wait until my Prince Charming finds me the way yours found you."

Twice.

He found me twice. I am the luckiest woman in the world.

We can't change what's already happened. We can only accept it and embrace the future.

Once Gage is back in New York, I'll share my past with him so we can start building a new tomorrow together.

***

Gage: *I have some legal stuff to deal with here. I'll be back in New York ASAP.*

"You look worried," Tilly notes as she slathers soft butter onto a piece of bread. "Is it about Gage?"

I haven't told Tilly or Olivia that Gage isn't Kristin's biological father.

All they know is that he's been in California visiting his daughter for the past week.

I watch as Tilly takes a big bite of the bread. "Someone is starving."

She chews, swallows and then answers, "I haven't eaten anything yet today."

It's noon and we're waiting for two big bowls of pasta at a restaurant around the corner from my store.

The only thing that I've consumed today is a cup of lukewarm coffee, even though I've been up since six.

My communication with Gage has been sparse and interrupted by my work.

We talked on the phone once but that was two days ago and it was brief.

I could hear Kristin in the background calling to him, so I made an excuse about needing to get to the showroom floor. I didn't want to steal a minute away from his time with his daughter.

I expected Gage to come back today, but the text message he just sent rained on that parade.

I type back a response to him as Tilly finishes her bread and butters another slice.

Kate: *I'll see you when you get here.*

As much as I want to pry and question what's going on there, I don't want to insert myself into the middle of a situation that I don't belong in.

I haven't met Kristin yet and the conversations I've had with Gage about her have only touched on where things stand in terms of his right to custody and visitation.

All I do know is that something has shifted.

He's in the same city as his daughter now and lawyers are involved. That has to be good news.

Chapter 50

Gage

A man can wish for many things in his life.

Health.

Happiness.

Wealth.

Love.

I've had every last one of them.

My good health is a gift. Happiness has eluded me at times. Wealth was there until it was stripped from me when I dropped out of medical school. My parents donated my trust fund to a worthwhile charity since I wasn't in line to follow the dream they had for me.

Love is the most complex in my life.

I have loved one woman. I still love her with every cell of my being.

My heart beats for her. My future belongs to her.

Yet, here I am, at the East River wondering what the hell I'm supposed to do next.

I touched down at La Guardia an hour ago.

I went home and then hit the sidewalk in running shorts and shoes.

This is where I landed, looking out over the water that used to be my oasis.

Katie is that now.

I want to be that for her, but I don't know if life is going to allow it.

Madison is set on settling down in Los Angeles. She's looking for a job and a place to live.

Perry is hanging back to start a new life in London, so Madison agreed to grant me as much time as I want with Kristin.

Her plan is simple.

I move into a place close to them and we pick up where we left off in Nashville before Perry dropped back into the picture.

Kristin will still visit him twice a year, but Madison and I will be her caregivers.

It's not going to be easy since I've built a life in Manhattan.

I spot Gus walking toward me. I raise a hand in greeting. He responds in kind.

"You've been MIA." He pats my shoulder as he passes behind me on his way to the bench. "Where did life take you, Gage?"

"Back to California."

"You went to see your folks?"

Gus knows I grew up out west. I haven't gotten into the details about my complicated relationship with my parents.

They love their granddaughter.

They'd love their son more if he were a doctor and not a bartender.

"My daughter," I correct him taking a seat next to him.

"Kristin."

I'm surprised that he remembers her name.

"How's your girl?" He taps my knee. "I bet she's growing like a weed."

He's never seen a picture of her. He has no idea how old she is yet he's interested.

I suspect that stems from the lack of a family in his life.

"She'll be as tall as me soon," I joke.

"Time slips by in the blink of an eye." He winks at me. "How's Katie been?"

Supportive. I'd bet my last dollar that she's also confused and concerned.

I need to see her. I have to explain where things stand with Kristin.

"Beautiful." I smile at him.

"Bring her around." He crosses his legs. The hem of his pants slides up, revealing a brown sock with holes.

His shoes look to be about a size nine.

I store that to memory so I can pick up a raincoat and socks. A sun hat wouldn't hurt on mornings like this.

"You'll be here tomorrow?" I ask as I push to stand.

"If that's God's plan you'll find me here." He gazes out over the water. "Whatever is troubling you, look to Katie for the answer."

"Who says I'm troubled?"

He looks up into my face. "It's not just words that tell a story, Gage. Your eyes give you away."

I shove a hand at him. "You're the wisest man I've ever know, Gus."

He takes my hand in both of his. "You're the kindest I've ever met so I'd say we're even."

***

I watch through the glass window at the front of Katie Rose Bridal as Katie consoles Annalise.

I'm not shocked that she's back with her wedding gown in her hands. I am surprised that she's here this early. The store doesn't open for another twenty minutes.

Some might say it's my fault that Annalise is facing the end of her engagement, but I did what needed to be done.

I called Myles when I was in Los Angeles, and we talked.

I reminded him about my mistakes with Katie and the loss that I carried with me for years.

He brushed it off, telling me that his situation is different than mine.

I pulled out the big guns and brought up the bachelor party.

I asked him to consider Annalise in this and whether it was fair to marry her if he still loved Karen.

He told me to mind my own fucking business.

Katie glances at the windows, her gaze catching on me. She looks beautiful in the white dress she's wearing. Her hair is pulled up into a high ponytail.

I give the handle on the door a tug. It's unlocked so I walk in.

"That's a great idea, Kate. I'll donate the gown today. I love the idea of someone else having a chance to wear it," Annalise says before she looks in my direction. "Gage?"

"Annalise," I answer back.

She drops the gown and rushes at me, launching into my arms. "Thank you. Thank you a million times over."

I step back to study her face. "Thank you?"

She glances back at the crumpled dress on the floor. "I knew that he didn't love me, but I got so caught up in the idea of the big wedding, the gown, some kids in the future… all of it."

Katie moves closer to where we're standing. The expression on her face is unreadable.

Fuck. This can't be easy for her. I didn't leave her because I loved another woman, but still, she was left with a wedding dress and no groom to exchange vows with.

"Myles told me that you talked to him." Annalise wrings her hands together in front of her. The left is missing her massive engagement ring. "You told him to be honest with me, didn't you?"

"I told him to be honest with himself." I lock eyes with Katie. "I have some experience with that."

Annalise's gaze volleys between Katie and I. "I want a man who looks at me the same way you look at Kate. That's what I'm waiting for."

"You'll find it," I assure her.

"I hope you two know how lucky you are." She looks to Katie before her eyes land on me. "One day you're going to make beautiful babies together."

A pained sound escapes Katie as her hands dart to her face.

Her knees give out, but I'm on her before she reaches the floor. I scoop her into my arms and carry her to a bench.

"I'm going to go," Annalise whispers somewhere behind us.

Katie sobs into my shoulder. "I'm sorry, Gage. I'm so sorry."

For what? What the fuck does this woman have to be sorry for?

"No," I whisper as I hold her against me. "I'm sorry. I'm the one who fucked up the best thing that ever happened to me."

"I'm sorry," she whimpers.

"Katie." I cup my hands around her face, forcing her to look at me. "You have nothing to be sorry for."

Her bottom lip trembles as she stares into my eyes. "Please forgive me."

"For what?" I spit out as tears cloud my vision.

What the fuck is going on?

Her voice is strangled as it leaves her lips. "I lost our baby, Gage. It's my fault that our baby died."

Chapter 51

Kate

Fear has more power in the darkness than in the light.

My mom only said that to me once. It was six weeks after I arrived in Manhattan.

I had called her in a panic one afternoon. She thought I was crying about Gage. She told me that she knew that I was scared about the next steps in my life, but that I'd make it through if I tackled it head-on.

She was offering advice about my broken heart, but I was facing something life-changing.

My heart was still aching from the loss of my fiancé, but in a free clinic, three blocks from my apartment on the Upper West Side, a doctor with a graying beard and a thick Scottish accent told me that I was going to be a mom.

I'd missed my period.

I didn't notice at first, but when it dragged into the next month and I realized that I hadn't bought tampons since I moved to New York, I knew something wasn't right.

I attributed it to not eating right, or stress.

I expected to walk out of the clinic with a stern warning about taking better care of myself.

Instead, I walked out with a new feeling in my chest.

It was a different kind of love than what I'd felt for Gage.

This was peppered with hope and sprinkled with a fierce need to protect.

I wanted that baby more than I wanted anything other than to be Gage's wife.

Just a few weeks later, in a hospital uptown, my dream to be a mom ended after I started bleeding.

Fear has kept me from telling anyone, until today.

"You were pregnant?" Gage's gaze drops to the front of my dress. "When?"

"I found out after I moved here." I glance down at the floor. "The doctor said that sometimes the pill doesn't work if you're sick. I had caught a cold."

"After we went for that walk in the rain."

I nod. "I took some cold medicine. It did something to my birth control."

He turns his head, staring out the front windows of the boutique. "A baby. Our baby."

"The doctor said it was best to wait to tell anyone until I was three months along." I push the words out in haste, trying to crowd everything that I've wanted to say into a few short sentences. "I didn't tell anyone. No one knew."

His head snaps back. "You didn't tell anyone?"

I was mindful of what the doctor said, but it was a secret that I cherished.

I would spend hours in my apartment thinking about baby names, and where I'd put the crib in my bedroom.

I window shopped at a baby store two blocks from here.

I'd stand in front of the display every day, cataloging in my mind everything I needed and wanted for my baby.

"I was almost twelve weeks when…" I hold back a sob. "I tried my best to take care of him. I wanted to take care of him forever."

His control breaks right in front of me. I see it. "It was a boy?"

I slide my fingers over my cheeks to push away my tears. "It was too early for a sonogram, but I knew. I just knew it was a boy."

"Our boy." He closes his eyes. "Our little boy."

"Something happened one morning."

I've relived that moment in my mind every day since. It was raining. I was wearing heels. I was hurrying. I ran into a woman on the sidewalk.

I stumbled but didn't fall.

Later that day at work, I saw blood in my panties.

The doctor in the emergency room told me that there wasn't a heartbeat. She tried to comfort me by explaining it wasn't my fault and that bumping into a stranger's shoulder wasn't what caused my baby to die.

"What happened?" Concern knits his brow.

"The doctor said that sometimes a baby's heart just stops beating. I almost fell that morning. I thought that was why."

"No." His hands jump to my face. "Jesus, Katie, no. It wasn't your fault."

"I would have traded my life for the baby's life." I can't hold in a sob.

His lips brush mine. "I should have been with you. I could have taken care of you after. You were all alone?"

I nod.

"I can't fucking believe you went through this by yourself." He holds me against his chest. "You needed me. I should have never left your side."

Chapter 52

Gage

Katie has been fast asleep since I tucked her into her bed.

Seven or eight hours have passed since I brought her home from the boutique after telling Natalie that she needed to cover for Katie today.

I've been next to the woman I love, watching her sleep while I think about the hell she went through.

I can't be angry that she didn't tell me she was pregnant with my child. All I feel is compassion.

I left her. I didn't tell her why so when she found out she was expecting a baby, her emotions must have been twisted into such a tangled knot that she couldn't unwind them.

She was expecting my child.

I shake the thought away with a heavy exhale.

"Gage," she whispers, her eyes still closed. "Are you here?"

I lean forward on my forearm so I can press a kiss to her mouth. "I'm not going anywhere."

Her hand snakes behind my head to twist in my hair. She kisses me. This time it's soft with parted lips. "There's something else I need to tell you."

"Open your eyes," I whisper against her mouth.

"I'm scared to."

I manage a small laugh. "Tell me every secret that's inside of you. I want to know them all."

"I only have one more," she says, her eyes still shut tight.

"Open your eyes and tell me."

Her eyelids flutter, revealing those two beautiful hazel eyes.

"The secret, Katie. I want to know."

I pray to God it's not as earth shattering as the one she told me this morning. I'm still processing that. It's going to take days, if not weeks, for me to wrap my mind around the fact that she was pregnant.

Her hand slides to my cheek. "I love you."

I've waited five years for that priceless gift. "I love you too."

"You'll tell me about Kristin." Her eyes search mine. "Tell me everything."

"You need to sleep more." I run my hand over her forehead. "Sleep. I'll make us dinner and then we'll talk."

"Just another five minutes," she says, snuggling into my neck.

I'll take it.

I'm due back in California the day after tomorrow to sign the new custody agreement. I won't leave Katie, but I can't miss my chance to have unrestricted access to my daughter.

In a perfect world, I'd see my daughter every day while I built a future with the woman I love.

I don't live in a perfect world.

I live in a complicated world full of challenges. I'll make it all work. I have to.

***

"I haven't slept this much in years." Katie looks up at me.

I'm back in bed.

I spent most of my afternoon on the phone talking to my daughter, her mother and my attorney.

Kristin wanted to know when she'd be able to visit me in New York.

Madison shut that down quickly, saying that she needed to find a job before they could plan another trip.

They're still living under my parents' roof.

I suspect that will stay the same until Madison can set herself up in a small place.

"How long have you been awake?"

I planned on being here when she opened her eyes, but I was in the kitchen prepping a salad while I semi-argued with Madison about the future.

I kept the tone of my voice down not just so I wouldn't wake Katie, but I didn't want to get Madison fueled up.

Kristin's been through enough. She doesn't need the added stress of listening to us debate what's best for her future.

"Not long," she answers with a smile.

"You've been carrying the weight of the world on your shoulders for years." I brush my lips over her forehead. "I wish I had known what you went through."

Her hand leaps to my face to cradle my cheek.

"I'll do everything in my power to take care of you now," I go on, "I love you, Katie."

"I love you," she whispers back. "I'm so happy that you're here."

236

I move so I'm closer to her. I know she can feel the brush of my hard cock against her hip.

"You're happy that you're here too," she sighs. "I've missed you."

I'm about to show her just how badly I've missed her.

Chapter 53

Kate

Gage's fingers slide over my hip before they dive between my legs.

He groans when he feels how wet I am.

"Jesus, Katie," he growls out between clenched teeth. "I could blow my load just from touching you."

"I want more," I say shamelessly kicking back the covers that are shielding my body from his view.

"More," he repeats back, gliding down my body. He peppers kisses over my skin.

First, it's my breasts.

He stops to take my left nipple between his teeth. When he bites, I purr.

"You like that?"

He knows I do.

His attention and talented tongue shifts to my right breast. He sucks the nipple between his lips.

I arch my back from the bed when he captures my left nipple between his fingers.

He pinches it, just as he bites my other nipple.

I scream out.

"I can't wait to taste you." He licks my nipple softly, lashing his tongue against it. "You're going to be so wet."

His mouth moves to my stomach. He takes his time kissing the skin and biting it.

By the time he reaches the top of my mound, I'm squirming and whimpering.

"You'll come as soon as I touch your pretty little clit." He pushes my legs apart, revealing my bare pussy.

"Please, Gage," I whine. "Please."

His head drops, but it's not to my core. He sets his attention on my inner thighs.

Painfully slow kisses dot my skin as he nears the top of my right thigh.

"I can see how wet you are." He blows on my pussy. "You're going to come over and over again."

I reach down to cup my hand over the back of his head, urging him closer.

His tongue moves in one long stroke over my core.

I scream out in pained pleasure. The ache for release is too much. "Lick me."

"Lick you?" he repeats back with a note of amusement laced into his tone. "You're so fucking polite. Tell me what you really want."

I look down into his stormy green eyes.

"Eat my pussy. Make me come."

He lowers his head and sends me almost instantly into a mind-numbing climax.

***

"I doubt like hell that I can walk." Gage's laughter fills the room. "You've fucked the life right out of me."

"I was returning the favor." I cup my hand over my mound. "My pussy is aching more now than before you fucked me."

He turns to look at me. "I like when you talk dirty."

I kiss him softly on the mouth. "I love when you do."

"In that case…" He turns on his side to face me. "I love fucking you. I love how tight your pussy is. I love that you get so wet that I can taste you on my lips for hours after."

"You're going to make me want you again." I sigh.

"I want you to feel that forever."

"I will."

"Let's get you up." He rolls onto his back. "I made a salad earlier. You should eat some of that and then let me wash you in the shower."

I swing my legs over the side of the bed. Spotting my blue silk robe on the floor, I reach for it. "Do you remember when you used to wash me in the shower?"

Silence fills the room.

"You'd pretend that you wanted to soap me up, but it was a ploy to feel me up."

There's still no response. Glancing over my shoulder, I see him standing with his phone in his hands.

"Is everything all right, Gage?"

His head pops us. "Everything is perfect. I'm with the woman I love."

"I'll meet you in the kitchen." I move to stand. "Take your time."

I tie the sash on the robe and walk out of the room, knowing that everything is far from all right.

Chapter 54

Gage

"It's not my birthday." Gus looks down into the brown paper shopping bag that contains a new raincoat, four pairs of socks, a pair of new shoes and a sun hat.

"It will be one day this year," I quip. "Call it a friend doing another friend a favor."

"I'll call it what it is." He places the bag on the bench. "You're a saint."

"Far from it." I laugh.

I don't know what the hell I am.

Selfish fits the bill.

I left Katie last night so I could stop in at Tin Anchor. I bought the bar months ago as a way to build something for my daughter.

The plan has never been to get her behind the bar serving drinks once she's old enough.

I wanted to double or triple my investment in the place so I could leave her something when I'm gone.

I named it after her.

The first time I called her Tin, her face lit up, so it stuck.

She's been my anchor in the storms of my life these past five years. She kept me grounded when all I wanted to do was bolt.

I don't want to give up the bar, but I might have to in order to fund bi-monthly cross-country trips to see Kristin.

"Trouble has found its way back to you." Gus pats my shoulder. "What's weighing you down?"

I shove my hands into the pockets of my jeans.

I didn't feel up to working out this morning, so I put on the jeans and a Tin Anchor shirt. I needed kindness more than exercise. I knew Gus could provide it.

The urge to swing by Katie's place to see her first was strong, but she told me in an early morning text message that she's meeting Tilly and Olivia for breakfast.

I scrub a hand over the back of my neck. "Kristin and her mom are setting up shop in California. Katie is here."

Gus pushes the paper bag to the side before he lowers himself to the bench. "What's Katie's take on this?"

I've been hesitant to throw this at her.

I turned her life inside out once.

How the fuck can I ask her to do it again?

"Don't tell me you haven't discussed it with her." Gus waves a finger at me.

"I can't expect her to sacrifice everything for me, Gus."

"You think it's a sacrifice. Katie may see it differently."

"I can do both coasts. I spend weekdays here, and a few times a month fly back there."

"That sounds like a hell of a bad idea to me."

"Why?" I ask with a cock of my brow. "It can work."

"Until Kristin takes ill and you're clear across the country." He jabs a finger into my side. "Or you burn out because you're running yourself ragged trying to live two lives at once."

I turn to look at him. "If I ask Katie to move back to California with me, she'll be giving up her business and her friends. She's made a good life for herself here."

"If you don't ask her to move to California with you, you'll be taking away her choice." He glances at the river. "You don't get to decide what's best for her, Gage. She does."

He's right. I made a choice for Katie years ago that changed both of our lives forever. I can't do it again.

***

Hours later, I watch Katie through the window of her bridal store.

She's wearing a light green dress. Her hair is braided to the side. She's breathtaking, as she always is.

A smile lights up her face. Pure joy emanates from her when she's around a bride-to-be. I can't imagine the inner strength it took for her to get through the days after I called off our engagement.

On top of that, she had to face losing our baby on her own.

She pushed through. She prospered. She came out of it with grace and humility.

She's the woman that I want my daughter to look up to.

Madison is a good mom, but I want Katie's influence in Kristin's life.

I'll only get that if I tell Katie what's going on. I have to let her in. I have to give her a voice in this because it's the right thing to do.

My phone chimes in my pocket.

I tug it out and glance at the screen.

It's a text message from Madison.

I read it twice, not believing for a damn minute that it's real.

Madison: *Cancel ur flight to L.A. Ur not coming here.*

I turn my back to the windows of Katie Rose Bridal so the woman I love doesn't see the rage on my face.

With fury racing through me, I dial Madison's number.

"Hello, Gage," she says in that smug tone I can't fucking stand.

"What the hell? We had an agreement. I am coming to see my daughter."

"Calm the fuck down." She laughs. "You're not coming here because we're coming there tomorrow."

"You're coming here?" I turn back to face the windows of Katie's shop.

I spot her looking at me. A beautiful smile graces her face.

Calmness blankets me when she raises her hand to wave.

I do the same back.

"Don't read too much into this," Madison stops to take a deep breath. "I got a call from a company in New York today. It's a huge company, Gage. I have an interview for a District Operations Manager position."

"In Manhattan?" I ask to be crystal clear.

"In Manhattan," she repeats back. "I'm qualified for it. It's right up my alley and it would make things easier for Kristin."

I respect her for wanting to put our daughter's needs first.

"It's closer to Perry too, so fingers crossed."

"I'll arrange a hotel for you and Kristin," I offer because I want my daughter to be comfortable.

"I already booked a room for myself." She clears her throat. "Kristin can stay with you if you want."

If I want?

"What the fuck do you think?" I chuckle. "Let me know your flight details. I'll meet you at the airport."

"I hope I get the job," she says quietly. "I never considered Manhattan as a place to live full-time, but maybe this is meant to be."

"You didn't say a word about applying for a job here." I stare at Katie, wanting nothing more than to go into the store and sweep her into my arms.

"I didn't apply for it." Madison laughs. "The woman who called me said she heard from a friend of a friend that I was looking for a job and wondered if I'd be interested in relocating to New York City. I've told everyone I know out here that I'm searching so I guess someone put in a good word."

Fate doesn't have a hand in this.

It's too big of a coincidence.

"What's the name of the company?"

"Liore Lingerie. The woman I'm meeting is named Olivia Donato."

Chapter 55

Kate

"I need to talk to you," I say to Gage as he marches toward me.

He's been outside my store for the last ten minutes. He spent most of that time on the phone.

I couldn't hear anything he was saying, but I know what it's about.

Yesterday, when he thought I was asleep in my bed, I was listening to him.

He was telling Kristin that he loved her and hoped that one day he could show her Times Square and the Empire State Building.

She must have handed the phone back to Madison because his tone changed before he said that he wanted them in Manhattan.

Once that call ended, he spoke to his attorney for more than thirty minutes.

Half-way through that discussion, I knew what I needed to do.

It's what I want to do.

I've already set the wheels in motion so I can move back to California and build a life with Gage.

I had breakfast this morning with my two best friends so I could break the news to them.

They cried. I wept, but we promised each other that we'd do video chats every day and I'd fly back to Manhattan as often as I can to see them.

Olivia had a million questions about Kristin and her mom.

Tilly was silent, lamenting the fact that I won't be around to drink martinis with her and share sandwiches at lunch.

I'll miss them.

They're like sisters to me, but Gage is my love.

Kristin is his daughter. He needs to be with her and I need to be where he is.

"I need to talk to you," he says once he's in front of me. "I fucking love you. Do you know how much I love you?"

I can't answer because I'm swept into his strong arms. He spins us in a circle before he lowers me and takes me into his arms for a deep, sensual kiss.

I hear a smattering of applause from the customers in the showroom.

"Gage," I say his name on a sigh. "I have to say something."

"Let me be your husband."

"Oh my God," Natalie screams from the right. "Is this a proposal?"

Gage huffs out a laugh. "That's coming, but this is a promise that I'm going to honor and cherish this woman until I die."

"I love you," I say, my head spinning. I can't tell if it's from him picking me up or his words. "We need to talk about California."

"We need to thank Olivia," he answers back.

"Olivia?" I feel like we're having two different conversations. "What does Olivia have to do with anything?"

His hands cup my cheeks. "You don't know?"

"I don't know what?"

"Natalie, you'll keep an eye on the store, won't you?" Gage glances over at her. "I need to take the woman I love to see her best friend."

***

"Oh, shit." A smile blooms on Olivia's lips when looks up from her desk and sees us. "I'm busted, aren't I?"

Gage drops my hand and starts across Olivia's office. "You're a fucking lifesaver."

"I'm a woman who wants the best for everyone." She stands and embraces him.

My gaze volleys from Gage to Olivia. "Will someone tell me what's going on? Does this have to do with us moving to California?"

That turns Gage on his heel to face me. "You were going to move to California with me?"

"Of course I was," I say without hesitation. "I love you. I want to be with you. I'd move anywhere to be with you."

Olivia brushes past me to close her office door. "I'm going to interrupt because I know how this looks."

"It looks like you want to keep Katie in New York." Gage moves to wrap his arm around my shoulder.

"I don't understand what's happening." I look up at Gage before I shift my gaze to Olivia. "Tell me, Liv."

She takes a step closer to us. Scooping both my hands into hers, she smiles. "This morning you told Tilly and me that you loved him more than anything."

I nod. "I did say that because I do."

"You also said that you overheard him talking on the phone yesterday."

I blush at her admission. I look up at Gage. "I didn't mean to overhear."

"I'm damn glad that you did." He leans down to kiss my forehead.

"I am too." Olivia gives my hands another squeeze. "You told me that Gage wants to stay in New York and that he wants to raise Kristin here."

"I did hear him say those things," I affirm with a nod of my head.

"I asked about Madison for a reason." Olivia drops my hands. "I was a little surprised that you didn't question me about why I wanted to know her last name."

I laugh. "You're a detail-oriented person."

"A few hours ago, I called and asked her to come to Manhattan to interview for a job here at Liore."

My breath catches in my chest. "You what?"

"I know it's not my place." She bows her head. "I'm not trying to interfere in anyone's life or dictate the future. I'm offering an alternative solution that will allow all of you to be in New York. Gage doesn't have to give up the business he's building. You don't have to give up the bridal boutique and Kristin can grow up in this amazing city."

I look at Gage. The smile on his face says it all. He's thrilled that Olivia put herself in the middle of this.

"I should also mention that Madison is overly qualified for the position I'm going to offer her." She tilts her head. "She has a business degree. She held a comparable position in Nashville for four years. I expect her to bring good things to the Liore team."

"Olivia." I move to hug her. "I can't believe you're doing this."

"I didn't put a whole lot of thought into it, Kate." She rests her hands on my shoulders. "I admit I'd be lost without you, but I offered her an interview because the position is vacant, she's qualified and I'm going to need a babysitter for Arleth in a few years and I think Kristin will make my short list of candidates."

There are no words to thank her for what she's done for me, and for Gage.

I take her back in my arms and pray that everything will work out just as it's supposed to.

Chapter 56

Gage

I've been waiting for this day for five years.

I hold tightly to Kristin's hand as we round the corner. The wind is whipping her hair around her face.

She took time choosing an outfit to wear.

She must have tried on everything in her suitcase twice before she settled on a pair of jeans and a red sweatshirt.

The sneakers on her feet are hot pink.

She looks like the beautiful nine-year-old child that she is. New York City agrees with her. It's only her fourth day here and she's already calling it home.

I slow my pace as we near Katie Rose Bridal.

It was Kristin's idea to come here. I told her that we'd be having dinner with Katie, but she wanted to see the store.

I called Katie an hour ago to ask if we could stop by.

She didn't hesitate for a second. She wants us here.

"Is this it?" Kristin looks up at the white awning that bears the name of the store.

"Katie Rose Bridal," she says quietly. "It's the prettiest name for a store."

I swing open the heavy glass door. "After you, my little lady."

"I'm not your little lady anymore." She giggles. "I'm taller than when you used to call me that."

"You'll always be my little lady."

"Is that her?" Kristin tugs on my arm. "That lady with the blonde hair over there. Is that her, Daddy?"

I look over to where Katie is standing. She's wearing a simple black sheath dress. Her long hair is cascading down her back in waves.

"That's Katie," I say with a sigh. "Let's go say hello."

***

"If I ever get married, I'm coming here." Kristin touches the lace of the train of a cream colored gown. "There are a million dresses in your store, Katie."

Katie looks to me. I know she's on the verge of crying.

It started an hour ago when I introduced my daughter to her. Katie held out her hand, but Kristin ignored it and went in for a hug.

Katie clung to her as her eyes met mine.

It was one of the defining moments of my life and I lost it.

I had to turn around to shield my daughter from the rush of emotions I felt.

We've spent our time since on a tour of the store, drinking soda, and talking about the subjects that Kristin most loves in school.

English and Math.

I need to brush up on both if I'm going to help her with her homework.

"My mom got a job here." Kristin smiles. "Do you know what that means?"

Katie taps her index finger to her chin. "It means we can drink soda again?"

Kristin lets out a belly laugh. "No. It means I get to live with my Daddy again."

"Your dad is very lucky." Katie takes a seat on the bench next to Kristin.

We're at the back of the showroom, away from a large bridal party that is swooning over a rack of gowns that Natalie rolled out of the stockroom.

"Can I tell you something?" Kristin rests her hand on Katie's knee.

"Anything."

"My Daddy used to tell me stories about Katie. He loved her with his whole heart." She leans closer to Katie, her voice dropping to a whisper. "I think he was talking about you."

I lean closer to my daughter. "I was."

"Do you want to marry her, Daddy?"

"Very much."

Kristin scratches her cheek. "So ask her."

"I will one day," I tell her. "When the time is right."

Katie smiles at me.

Kristin's gaze volleys from my face to Katie's. "I think she'll say yes if you ask now. I saw you put the ring in your pocket this morning."

I did put it there so when the moment felt right, I could drop to my knee and ask the question to the love of my life again.

"Daddy Perry asked me if he could have Mommy's hand and my hand in marriage, and I said yes." She reaches for my hand. "I say yes that Katie can have our hand in marriage too."

The question has been waiting to be asked since I walked into this store weeks ago and saw my beautiful Katie again after years of being apart.

I look at Katie for guidance, but I see my love reflected in her eyes.

I slide to the floor on bended knee.

Kristin is on her feet and next to me, before I have a chance to tug the silver band with the blue topaz stone out of my pocket.

Once the ring is in my palm, I look at the love of my life.

"Katie," I say her name quietly. "From the first moment I saw you eight years ago, my heart belonged to you. You are my true north. You are my beacon in the darkness. You are the light that will forever guide me home. You are my everything."

Kristin pats me on the shoulder. "Ask her. Say it."

"Katie Wesley, will you be my wife?"

"Yes," she says in a voice that speaks of the love and compassion that has always lived in her.

She's accepted me with all my flaws, through every fuck up and each fall I've taken.

She carried our baby, suffered through the loss alone, and still has a heart that accepts without question.

I can see the love she already has for my daughter in her eyes.

It will only multiply when we have our own children.

254

Kristin cups her hands around her mouth and screams. "We are getting married."

We are. As soon as my daughter is settled into her life in New York and Katie is ready, we'll say our vows to each other.

Vows that will last for eternity and will never be broken.

Epilogue

Six Months Later

Gage

"I've got a fiancée to see and a daughter to hug." I pat Gus on the back. "You'll keep those young ones in line if I take off, won't you?"

Zeke and Callie both flip me the bird.

Gus lets out a hearty laugh. "I've done my time for today, but I'm all for hanging around."

Five months ago Gus walked into Tin Anchor.

It wasn't fate that brought him to the door. It was the T-shirt I was wearing when I handed him a brown paper bag with a few items in it.

I had no idea at the time that I had struck up a friendship with Gustav Strand.

The man is a philanthropist and one of the richest men in the country.

He started a charitable foundation with his wife, Lois, years before his death.

He lives a modest existence so he can share his wealth with those who need it.

He came into Tin Anchor that night months ago to hand me a check to thank me for my kindness. He wanted to ease my financial burden by covering Kristin's future in college.

My parents set that up when she was four-years-old, so I asked Gus to donate the funds where he saw fit.

He took care of it, dividing the money between a homeless shelter in Queens and a community center in Morningside Heights that offers free dance lessons to seniors.

He's dropped in on a few classes since.

Three nights a week he stops by the bar to help out.

He makes a few drinks, tells a story or two, and keeps an eye on the place when I'm not around.

Zeke and Callie are qualified to do that, but it gives Gus a sense of purpose that he needs. I consider him family now.

He's sat down for a few meals with Katie, Kristin, and I.

"Go home." He points at the door. "I'll lock up the place."

I know he will. He'll take care of it as he's taken care of so many people in this city. The two people I want to take care of are waiting at home for me, so I grab my winter coat and set out into the snow.

***

"Katie and Tilly are going to help me paint my bedroom purple." Kristin wraps a pink scarf around her neck. "We're doing it on the weekend."

"Tilly is going to help." Katie adjusts the wool hat on Kristin's head before she plants a kiss in the middle of her forehead. "I'm going to watch from the sidelines."

"Purple?" I raise a brow.

Katie tugs on the bottom of the large white sweater she's wearing. "Purple is the best."

"The best." Kristin gives Katie a big hug before she wraps her arms around me. "I'll be back tomorrow after school."

"I'll be waiting for you by the steps of the school." I lean down to kiss my daughter's cheek. "Be good to your mom tonight."

"I'm always good to her."

A knock at the door sends Katie in that direction. She swings it open.

"Hey, Kate." Madison looks at my fiancée with a smile before she locks eyes with me. "Thank you for the extra time with her tonight, Gage. I know I promised she could stay over, but she wants to braid hair tonight."

Our custody agreement is clear.

Kristin spends half her time with me and the other half at her mom's apartment four blocks from here.

We don't follow a schedule. It's fluid. We let Kristin decide where she wants to be. She's mindful of how much we all love her, so she splits her time up evenly.

"Things are good with you?" I ask Madison the same question I always do.

"Really good," she answers with a smile.

She's happy. She's working hard at Liore. After she took the job, I told her about Katie's friendship with Olivia. She didn't care how she got the position. She was grateful for the opportunity to work for the largest lingerie chain in the country.

Her divorce is still a work-in-progress, but she's been shielding Kristin from the details.

Our daughter is set to leave in two weeks to spend ten days with Perry. Madison is taking the trip with her. She'll be hanging out in London working on Liore business.

"I love you guys," Kristin says as she follows Madison out of the apartment and into the hallway.

"We love you too," Katie and I say in unison before I close the door and turn to the woman who owns my heart.

We haven't set a wedding date yet, but we will.

After Katie moved in with me, life settled into calm perfection.

We cherish every moment we have together. Katie spends her days at the bridal boutique. I'm at Tin Anchor as much as I need to be.

We love our daughter completely and each other fiercely.

"What's on your mind?" I tilt my head and study her face. "There's a secret brewing in there?"

Her hands fist in front of her. "Why would you say that?"

"I know you."

"You love me."

"Endlessly," I say back.

"Make love to me."

"Is that a request or a demand?" I laugh.

She shrugs her shoulder. "Both?"

I go to her, taking her beautiful face in my hands. I study her eyes. Those expressive hazel eyes can't hide anything from me.

I've known for weeks what she's holding inside, but I know that her past is dictating her present.

She's scared.

She doesn't have to be.

Her body has changed since fall has turned to winter. Her hips are softer, her face fuller. Her breasts are heavier and her stomach has the slightest bump. It's just enough that I know that a new life is growing inside of her.

"Will you marry me in summer, Katie?"

She nods. "Summer will be perfect, love."

"We'll invite your family and mine. Gus and Natalie. Zeke and Callie." I kiss her softly. "Kristin will be my best person. Tilly and Olivia will fight over who is the matron of honor."

She laughs. "They'll both be matron of honor."

"Arleth will be the flower girl."

Her eyes lock on mine. "Someone else will be there."

I swallow past the lump in my throat. I can finally celebrate the fact that I'm going to be a father again.

"Who?"

She casts her eyes down. "I know that you know who."

I tilt her chin back up with a touch of my finger. "I want you to say it and I want you to understand that I know why you've waited to tell me."

She bites her bottom lip. "Our baby, Gage. Our beautiful little baby will be there too."

"Do you know if it's a boy or a girl, Katie?"

She points at a plain white envelope on the dining room table next to the vase of yellow roses I brought home for her yesterday. "I picked that up today. It will tell us if it's a boy or girl. I wanted you to open it."

I march across the room with shaking hands and pick up the envelope. "You didn't peek?"

"I went for a sonogram this morning to make sure everything was okay." She pats her stomach. "I'm almost fourteen weeks now. They could tell the gender of our baby."

I rip the fucking thing open and yank out the folded piece of paper.

I knew this day would come when we agreed that she'd stop birth control. I admit I was disappointed when she didn't get pregnant the first month we tried. Jesus, did we try.

We haven't talked about it since, agreeing to let nature take its course.

"I don't give a shit if it's a boy or a girl." I turn to face her. "If it's healthy that's all I care about."

"It's your child." She kisses me. "It's going to be healthy, and strong, and wise. It's going to have a kind heart and I hope it has your beautiful green eyes."

I look down at the paper. "Are you ready?"

"Ready." She gives me a brisk nod.

I unfold the paper, slowly and with purpose. I read the text; my eyes clouded with tears that reach beyond pure happiness.

"It's a boy."

"Our baby boy." She launches herself into my arms. "I can't wait to meet him."

I can't wait either. Hell, I can't wait for every tomorrow.

Fate put Katie Wesley in my path eight years ago. Love will keep me by her side today and forevermore.

Preview of Versus

A Standalone Enemies-to-Lovers Romance

I chose the woman I brought home with me last night for one reason and one reason only.

She looks like *her*.

It's the same with every woman I bring home with me.

They always look like *her*.

Light brown hair, sky blue eyes and a body that takes me to that place I crave. It's where I forget – *her* innocence, my cruelty, everything.

Last night was different.

This one didn't only look like *her*, she danced like *her*, spoke in a soft voice like *her,* and when she lost control on my sheets in that split second I live for, she made a sound that cracked my heart open. My heart; cold and jaded as it is, it felt a beat of something for this one.

She left before I woke up.

I need to forget about the woman from last night, just like I've forgotten every woman but the one who started me on this path to self-destruction.

I might have been able to if I wasn't standing in a crowded courtroom ready to take on the most important case of my career staring at the woman who crawled out of my arms just hours ago and into the role of opposing counsel.

I may be a high-profile lawyer, but her name is one I'd recognize anywhere.

The woman I screwed last night is the same one I screwed over in high school.

Court is now in session, and it's me versus *her*.

Chapter 1

Dylan

The world within Manhattan is its own beast. You learn that when you live here. When you claw your way around this city looking for something elusive.

For some, that's a job that will keep a roof over their heads.

For others, it's a relationship that will stand the test of time and weather the winds of change.

I have the first and no interest in the second.

My needle in the haystack is a particular type of woman.

I don't bother with blondes.

My cock has zero interest in redheads.

For me, it's all about the type of woman I see in front of me now.

Light brown hair, blue eyes, and a petite body that can move to the beat of the music.

Experience has taught me that if a woman can dance, she can fuck.

The woman I'm watching now is graceful, beautiful, and within the hour will be in my bed.

I slide off the bar stool and approach her. "I'm Dylan."

She taps her ear. "What was that?"

I lean in closer as she dances around me. "I'm Dylan, and you are?"

"Dancing." She breathes on a small laugh. "It's nice to meet you, Dylan."

"You've been watching me." I stand in place while the patrons of this club down around me, brushing against my expensive, imported suit.

She spins before she slows. "I could say the same for you."

I look down at her face.

Jesus, she's striking. Her eyes are a shade of blue, that particular shade of blue that always takes my breath away.

"We're leaving together tonight."

That cocks one of her perfectly arched brows. "You're assuming that I'm not leaving with someone else."

"You're here alone." I spin when she does to catch her gaze again.

The skirt of her black dress picks up with the motion revealing a beautiful set of legs. "Maybe I like being alone."

"Not tonight." I reach for her hand.

She slows before she slides her palm against mine. "Dance with me, Dylan."

I breathe out on a heavy sigh. I haven't heard those four words in years. I haven't danced in as long.

I pull her close to me, sliding my free hand down her back. "What's your name?"

"Does it matter?" She looks up at me.

It never does.

I dance her closer to an alcove, a spot where the crowd is thin and the music quieter.

Her body follows mine instinctively, our shared movements drawing the admiring glances of others.

She's letting me lead now, but the sureness of her steps promises aggression in bed.

"We're wasting time. "

Her lips curve up into a smile. "Foreplay comes in many forms."

"Is that what this is?" I laugh. "I want to fuck you."

She presses every inch of her body against me. "You will."

My cock swells with those words. "Now."

"Patience, Dylan." Her lips brush my jawline. "I promise this will be a night you'll never forget."

Coming soon

WISH – A Novel by Deborah Bladon

If you haven't read Tilly and Sebastian's love story yet, you'll find that in WISH.

My twenty-fifth birthday was just like the twenty-four before it.

I stood next to my identical twin sister as we blew out the candles on our shared birthday cake.

She wished for a healthy new baby to add to the family she already has with her husband.

I wished for my parents to stop asking me why I wasn't more like my twin.

When I get back to Manhattan after my birthday trip, a surprise is waiting for me.

A tall, gorgeous, tattooed stranger is in my apartment.

Did I mention he's naked?

He says it's not a big deal. I say *it* is a BIG deal, if you know what I mean.

I assume he's here to see my roommate, but apparently I'm wrong since she left town while I was away.

Sebastian Wolf *is* my new roommate.

I'm tempted to throw him out after the first day, but I agree to give him another chance.

When I start to wish for more, I discover that my new roommate isn't the man I thought he was.

Chapter 1

Tilly

I can't look away.

I know that I should. I realize that it's the right thing to do, but my gaze stays locked on the sight that's in front of me.

It's an intricate tattoo that covers the broad left shoulder of a man. The sharp lines of dark ink dip down to curl around his muscular bicep.

The ink on his skin isn't the only mesmerizing thing about him. This man is not only tall and dangerously good-looking, but he's hung. As in, the-largest-cock-I've-ever-seen hung.

The stranger in my apartment isn't wearing any clothes. He's completely naked and standing next to the now dead bouquet of flowers that were delivered to me before I boarded a flight to San Francisco five days ago.

His eyes are closed, his phone is in his hand, ear buds are tucked in place, and he's swaying slowly to what must be music I can't hear.

I should walk over to him and tap him on the shoulder, but I can't.

My feet have been planted in this spot, just inside the foyer of my apartment since I got home a few minutes ago.

My roommate, Lisa, wasn't expecting me to come back for another three days.

We don't keep in touch when one of us is out of town. We barely speak when we pass each other in the hallway.

Lisa and I are not friends.

We're roommates; nothing more and nothing less.

She has every right to invite a guy over. We only have one unspoken rule. I don't knock if her bedroom door is closed, and she does the same if mine is shut.

This is the first time I've ever caught a glimpse of one of the men she's sleeping with. It was worth the wait. This man is ridiculously hot.

I have to cross the room so I can get to the hallway that leads to my bedroom. I need to do that without the naked stranger noticing me. The last thing I want is to make small talk with Lisa's lover right now.

I finally pull my gaze away from him to look down at the hardwood floors. I need to think. I know the sight of Lisa's latest is jumbling my thought process. It's understandable though. Who wouldn't have trouble focusing when an incredibly attractive naked man is across the room?

"Matilda?"

I close my eyes when I hear the distinctive rumble of a deep voice. Why does this man's voice have to sound so damn sexy?

I've never corrected Lisa about my name. Matilda Jean Baker is my full name, so my lawyer used it for the rental agreement I had Lisa sign before she moved in. Almost everyone, other than my boss, calls me Tilly.

I admit I like that the naked stranger is calling me Matilda, although I'm shocked Lisa bothered to mention me to him.

My eyes open and I try to focus on the phone in my hand. It's a stall tactic. I'm hesitant to look up again. I've already got a mental image of his body. I doubt I'll ever forget it.

"That's me." I sigh.

I hear his footsteps as he nears me.

Dammit. The naked stranger is almost right in front of me.

"I thought you were going to be in San Francisco until Sunday."

"I came home early," I say evenly.

I eye his bare feet. I know eventually I need to look up, but he's so close now and I don't trust myself not to stare at his dick. From this vantage point, I'll be able to see every vein and how wide the crown is.

"Matilda, are you okay? You're trembling." His hand brushes against my shoulder. "It's freezing outside. Did you come from the airport dressed like that?"

He's one to talk. At least I'm wearing clothes. The ripped jeans and old red college T-shirt I'm wearing did nothing to protect me from the blast of winter weather that arrived while I was gone. When I left last week, it was forty degrees warmer than it is now.

"I'll make some coffee."

My head darts up when he makes that announcement. Who offers to make a pot of coffee at two a.m. when they're wearing nothing and their lover is probably waiting in her bedroom for another round?

My gaze skims over his smooth chest until it lands on the faux fur blanket he's wrapped around his waist. His left hand is resting on his hip, the blanket's edges bunched into his fist.

"I didn't startle you, did I?" He looks down and into my eyes. "It's dark in here. You probably didn't even notice I was standing over there until I said your name."

It's not that dark.

He's unaware that I was staring at him when I first walked in. That means I won't have to awkwardly try and explain to my roommate why I was checking out her nude lover.

At least now he's grabbed the blanket from where it's usually placed over the back of the leather couch. I use that blanket to wrap around myself when I watch my favorite shows in the evening. Now, I'll always think about the fact that it touched his naked body.

I shake that thought from my head. "I should get to bed. It's been a long day for me."

He nods. "I understand. There's nothing better than sleeping in your own bed after a trip."

I reach to pick up my suitcase before I head toward my bedroom. He's wrong. The only thing better than sleeping in my bed after my trip to San Francisco would be sleeping next to him. Although, after seeing him naked, sleep would be the last thing I'd want to do.

"It's been a pleasure meeting you, Matilda," he calls from behind me.

The pleasure is all mine. It's technically all Lisa's. She's the one who gets to enjoy what I just saw.

With any luck, I won't hear the two of them together. After the week I just had, the last thing I need is a reminder that there are men in the world who know how to a fuck a woman raw.

I have no doubt that the naked stranger in my living room is one of them.

Available now!

THANK YOU

Thank you for purchasing my book. I can't even begin to put to words what it means to me. If you enjoyed it, please remember to write a review for it. Let me know your thoughts! I want to keep my readers happy.

For more information on new series and standalones, please visit my website, www.deborahbladon.com. There are book trailers and other goodies to check out.

If you want to chat with me personally, please LIKE my page on Facebook. I love connecting with all of my readers because without you, none of this would be possible.
www.facebook.com/authordeborahbladon

Thank you, for everything.

ABOUT THE AUTHOR

Deborah Bladon has never read a romance hero she didn't like. Her love for romance novels began when she was old enough to board the bus, library card in hand to check out the newest Harlequin paperbacks. She's a Canadian by heart, and by passport, but you can often spot her in New York City sipping a latte and looking for inspiration for her next story. Manhattan is definitely her second home.

She cherishes her family and believes that each day is a gift for writing, for reading, and for loving.

21892258R00166

Printed in Great Britain
by Amazon